# THE JOURNEY TO FORGIVENESS

VERA SMETZER



LOVE INSPIRED
INSPIRATIONAL ROMANCE

FSC www.fsc.org MIX Paper | Supporting responsible forestry FSC® C021394

LOVE INSPIRED®
INSPIRATIONAL ROMANCE

Recycling programs for this product may not exist in your area.

ISBN-13: 978-1-335-52912-1

The Journey to Forgiveness



Love Inspired
22 Adelaide St. West, 41st Floor
Toronto, Ontario M5H 4E3, Canada
www.LoveInspired.com

HarperCollins Publishers
Macken House, 39/40 Mayor Street Upper,
Dublin 1, D01 C9W8, Ireland
www.HarperCollins.com

**Printed in Lithuania**

1 2 3 4 5 6 7 8 9 10 LIT 28 27 26 25

# Maggie saw Oliver's mood brighten. "Gram, you got a d-d-dog?"

Gram answered, "No. This isn't my dog, but he'll be visiting us for a little while."

"That's s-super," said Oliver, who knelt on the ground and threw his arms around the dog's neck.

Maggie was amazed. She didn't even know her son liked dogs.

"Who does he belong to?" Oliver asked as Hero slurped him on the cheek.

"That would be me," said Jake.

"He's w-w-wonderful," opined Oliver.

Jake nodded. "Oliver, I'm your Uncle Jake. Your father's brother. Do you remember me?" he asked gently.

Oliver's blue eyes widened. He stood up and took a step back.

"It's all right if you don't," Jake said. "We can get to know each other again while I'm here. And I think Hero here wants to get to know you, too." Hero wagged his tail.

"I have to go into town now," Jake said. "Maybe Hero could stay and get to know you."

Oliver nodded, keeping his eyes on the dog, who leaned against him.

Maggie saw her son visibly shudder. She had no idea why. Right now, she didn't want Oliver out of her sight. And it looked like Hero felt the same way. She was thankful for that.

**Vera Smetzer** lives with her husband in the beautiful state of Maine. She loves spending time at the coast and in the woodlands, and can't decide which one she loves the most. With degrees in behavioral science and creative writing, Vera feels blessed to now be able to pursue her dream of writing happily-ever-after stories for Love Inspired. Connect with her at www.Facebook.com/vera.smetzer.

**Books by Vera Smetzer**

**Love Inspired**

*The Journey to Forgiveness*

Visit the Author Profile page at LoveInspired.com.

Repent ye therefore, and be converted, that
your sins may be blotted out, when the times of
refreshing shall come from the presence of the Lord.
—*Acts* 3:19

Thanks be to God!

I am grateful for the Great Love Inspired Author Search of 2025! I am especially grateful to my editor, Melissa Endlich, for believing in Jake's story. And to the entire Love Inspired team. Everyone has been a joy to work with!

To my writer friends and cheerleaders who encourage and support me on this creative journey. You are all rays of sunshine in my life.

And to my husband, Michael. For understanding my late-night writing inspirations. For making me laugh at his sometimes outrageous plot suggestions. For his steady belief in me. And for the pumpkin custard he makes to celebrate writing accomplishments both big and small.

# *Chapter One*

Arriving home in the middle of the night in a tow truck with Hero, his one-hundred-and-thirty-pound Bullmastiff, wasn't exactly how Jake Madison thought he'd surprise his grandmother and sister. He opened the door, but before he could unbuckle his seat belt, Hero jumped out and took off running. He'd been cooped up for too long.

The porch light flickered a few times before it stayed on. *I'll need to tend to that.*

Gram stepped out of the house in her pink bathrobe and slippered feet. "Matt, I heard your truck. Jake? Is that really you? Welcome home!" When he reached the porch, she enveloped him in a big hug.

"Hello, Mrs. Madison," Matt Cyr called out from the cab as he shifted into gear. "Jake, good to see you again! I'll let you know what the parts will run you. We should get the old gang from high school together at the Wild Onion Diner sometime."

"Sounds good," Jake said.

Gram patted his arm. "You should have told us you were coming, boy!"

"Surprise," he said without much enthusiasm. "Hope it's okay I brought a four-legged buddy with me."

"Oh, I don't care a whit. I'm just glad you're here. Are you hungry?"

"No, Gram. Not really." His stomach felt rocky from the trip.

Could be the two Moon Pies he washed down with chocolate milk from the vending machine at the garage.

Jake whistled. Hero ran toward them. "Gram, this is Hero."

Gram bent down and rubbed behind Hero's ears. "Who's a good boy?" she crooned.

Jake grinned. Hero was totally smitten.

"Thanks, Gram. I'll just grab a couple sheets and head out to the guest house. Let you get back to bed."

"Ah, no."

"No?" Jake's brow creased.

"No, you can't sleep in the guest house."

"Sure, I understand. Zoe is out there. I'll take a bedroom."

"Your sister isn't in the guest house. She has the whole second floor. On the first floor, we added an additional bedroom for me off the living room."

Jake winced. That addition must have cost a pretty penny. He should have paid for it.

"I didn't know you were renting out the guesthouse to strangers."

"Not a stranger out there, boy. Family."

Jake shook his head a bit to clear it. *Who then?*

"Maggie and Oliver are staying there."

"Oh!" His breath hitched. "Visiting?"

"No, they live here now. Maggie took over running the farm."

*Wait. What?*

Jake's chest tightened. It seemed like everyone had surprises tonight. More than once on the trip from Kansas he had thought it was a good thing he didn't have to see Maggie and her son, Oliver, right away. He'd planned to talk to Gram and find out how they were doing first.

A splinter of anger stabbed him. His brother, Paul, should be here with them. He closed his eyes briefly; sorrow followed the anger. He ached to see his brother one more time.

Maggie. She'd been the love of his life before he left Maine after high school. Jake assumed she'd wait. But he learned she'd married his brother, Paul, soon after. He'd felt betrayed. Although he knew that didn't make sense. If they'd fallen in love, so be it. Heartbroken over the loss of Maggie, he'd stayed on the road as the lead guitarist for the country rock band No Caution, until he realized it wasn't the music he wanted to play. The road wasn't where he wanted to be.

He caught the end of what Gram was saying. "…Maggie tried hard after that fire."

"Fire? What fire?"

"Let's get you inside. I'll fill you in on everything," Gram said.

Inside, Jake slid his backpack off his shoulders.

He drew in a deep breath. The smell of cinnamon calmed him.

The same white porcelain bowl that held Gram's keys sat on the old maple table by the door. He remembered his sister Zoe jumping out from under the table and yelling "Boo!" when someone came in.

He realized his grandmother hadn't taken her eyes off him. He smiled. Her hair was white now, a few more lines visible on her face. But her blue eyes still held the same sparkle and warmth they always had.

"Gram," he said as he drew her into a long hug. He realized just how much he'd missed her.

He stepped back. All right, now he was ready to know more. "Gram, what fire?" he asked.

"They were living in North Carolina. After Paul passed, Maggie and Oliver lived in the apartment over the flower shop she managed. One night a fire took out the whole block. Shortly after, I felt God telling me to call her. I asked her what she really wanted to do and…listen, this can all wait. You're about to fall over!"

Jake could kick himself. This was awful. He had tried to stay in touch. Obviously not enough.

He swayed slightly from exhaustion.

"What about my old room in the attic?"

"That's all yours. I'll get some sheets. Might want to open up the windows and let it air out."

With bedsheets in hand, he lumbered up the creaky stairs to the third floor. He noticed the leafy green wallpaper had been replaced by a small rose pattern.

Stepping inside his old bedroom, he could see surprisingly well. Moonlight filtered in through the leaves of the trees outside. This room still gave him the feeling of being in a treehouse.

He opened the windows and surprised an owl perched on a branch.

After he made the bed, he barely remembered his head hitting the pillow.

The next morning, he tried to work out the kinks in his back and shoulders from being cooped up in the car on the road. He looked around his old room. Posters of rock musicians and his collection of striped rocks. Gram hadn't changed a thing except for a few boxes marked *Christmas* that were now under the eaves.

Looking out the window, it was a perfect July morning in Maine. Well, almost. He still had to face his sister. And now, Maggie and Oliver, as well.

This trip was important to him for so many reasons. The most important one being that he wanted to make amends to his family for leaving and then staying away so long.

After their mother's death, his father couldn't cope with his grief and was angry all the time. He left Jake and his brother and sister in their apartment. The three of them had waited for their father to return. When he didn't and they couldn't hide the fact they were on their own any longer, Jake had called Gram, who'd brought them all to the farm.

Jake had felt overwhelmed. When the offer had come to join the band, he knew he could send money to Gram and his siblings. He'd needed to get away, to breathe on his own.

He'd never intended to be gone so long.

Not from his siblings and certainly not from Maggie, the love of his life.

Now, he wanted, no, he needed to make it up to all of them. He felt that God had forgiven him for how he left and for what followed in his life after that. But he was still working on forgiving himself.

Gram had set out water and some pot roast in bowls on the floor for Hero, but he was nowhere to be found.

He'd been overwhelmed by so much news last night when he'd arrived. He should have called first. The last thing Jake wanted to second guess was his decision to return. Would he still have come home had he known Maggie and Oliver were here? He'd like to think so.

Jake never wanted to be like his father. But he'd done the same thing his father had done and left. The only difference was Jake stayed somewhat in touch.

It had been so late when he got in last night, he'd only snagged a few hours of sleep. He needed coffee.

Downstairs, he headed toward the sound of someone bustling around in the kitchen. Gram always was an early riser.

"Mornin'," he called out as he entered the kitchen.

Glass shattered as the coffeepot hit the floor.

Jake stopped short and shouted, "Don't move, Sis!"

"Jake?!" Zoe called out.

He grabbed the blue broom and dustpan from their usual spot. Zoe picked up the larger glass shards by hand.

"Does Gram know you're home?" Zoe asked.

"The way you just yelled out my name, I think the entire town knows," he joked as he emptied the glass into the trash.

"You should have told us you were coming!" Zoe chided.

"Turns out I'm no good at surprises. Matt drove me home in the tow truck."

"Tow truck? You broke down?"

"About an hour out of town. Got in after midnight. Gram met us on the porch."

"Us?"

As if on cue, Hero came trotting into the kitchen.

"Zoe, Hero. Hero, Zoe," Jake said.

He pulled out dog food from his backpack by the door and filled his bowl. He needed to get to town to buy some more food for Hero.

"That's a big dog." Zoe looked a little apprehensive.

"He's a sweetheart," said Jake.

Hero proved him right by pausing his meal and licking Zoe's hand.

"Okay then," she chuckled, patting his head.

"Caffeinated tea for you, Bro? Looks like you could use some."

"Thanks, yes." His little sister. All grown up. The dark-washed jeans and turquoise blouse were a far cry from the torn overalls he remembered her in. What was her life like now? Was she dating anyone? Did she still want to ride in the rodeo? It was all she'd talked about growing up. He felt a fresh pang of guilt when he realized she'd been the only one left behind to help Gram with the farm after he'd left.

"Good morning, you two! I see the coffeepot has met its demise," said Gram.

Jake got up to hug her. "Sorry about the late-night arrival. And I'll get you another coffeepot."

"Yes, Jake certainly knows how to make an entrance *and an exit*," Zoe said with emphasis.

"Zoe," Gram scolded.

Jake flinched. "It's okay, Gram, nothing more than I deserve." He hadn't anticipated this reunion would be easy. "Gram, did Hero sleep with you last night?"

"He did. Right beside the bed. He sounded just like the Boston and Maine train your grandfather worked on."

Zoe and Jake both laughed out loud.

"Way to make a good impression," Jake told Hero.

"Aren't you late for the office, Zoe?" asked Gram.

"Office?" Jake inquired.

"Maggie's Flower Farm. I do the accounting and scheduling of the employees who work for Maggie. Generally I jump in where needed, that kind of thing."

Jake took a sip of tea. *Interesting.*

"I've got it covered, Gram. Just texted Maggie. Everyone knows what to do today. Schedules are on the counter."

Gram nodded and turned to Jake. "So how long are you staying?" she asked.

"Awhile."

"Riiiight," said Zoe.

"No really, I am," he insisted.

"Sounds good," said Gram. "We can keep you plenty busy around here if you want things to do until God shows His plans for you."

Jake drew in a deep breath and let it whoosh out. "Thanks, Gram."

He was home to make amends to his family for the way he'd left. He'd stayed on the road too long with the country rock band No Caution. He hadn't been home since Paul's funeral.

Zoe piped up. "You look a little shaggy, Bro. Do you want a haircut?"

"Now? Here? You?" Jake asked, confused.

"Yes, yes, and yes," Zoe said.

Gram laughed. "Don't look so surprised, Jake. Zoe has a

cosmetology license. Does a pretty good job, if I do say so myself." She gave her white wavy hairdo a fluff.

"Okay, Zoe." His can't-cook and couldn't-care-less-about-fashion sister had spent two years in beauty school?

"I also have an accounting degree," said Zoe casually.

"Good for you, Zoe. Way to go!"

"C'mon," she beckoned. "Let's go to the living room. We'll set up there."

"I'll stay here and finish my tea," Gram said. "And avoid any carnage," she added mischievously.

Jake's head whipped back to Gram, who chuckled. He hoped he wouldn't regret this.

Zoe seemed to know what she was doing with her scissors and clippers. She snapped a salon cape in the air and draped it over Jake.

"So, you work for Maggie?" Jake asked.

"Yes."

He tried again. "And she and Oliver live in the guest house now?"

"Yep."

"How is Oliver doing? He must be what? Nine now?"

"Eleven. Just had a birthday last month. We had a small family party for him," said Zoe as she moved to cut the hair on the back of his head.

"And?"

Zoe blew out an exasperated sigh. "And what?"

"How's he doing?"

"Okay. For the most part," said Zoe as she kept trimming.

"Something I should know?" asked Jake.

"Oliver is a good kid. He's…quiet." Zoe said nothing more.

Jake was definitely picking up a vibe about their nephew. It had to have been devastating for the boy to lose his father. And for Maggie to lose her husband. He should have been here for them as well as his gram and sister.

With God's help, he would try to make it up to them both.

* * *

Maggie had overslept.

She and her son, Oliver, lived at the far end of the flower fields in a renovated building that was supposed to be rented out for additional income. But after the North Carolina fire, Gram had offered it to them. A day didn't go by when Maggie wasn't grateful.

Hearing Oliver's bedroom door close, she remembered mornings when he would laugh and slide past her in his stocking feet, playing air guitar. She still had some good memories of life in Chapel Hill, North Carolina.

Maggie hurried downstairs and saw Oliver zipping up his backpack in the hallway.

"Honey, you should have woken me," she said.

"Mom, I—I was f-f-fine. You need your rest," he told her.

A minivan pulled up out front, and the driver honked once.

"Bye, Mom." He gave her a hug.

"Bye, honey. Have fun at camp. Love you." She stood in the doorway and waved. Oliver as well as a couple of the other kids waved back.

Maggie wished her son hadn't had to endure so much in his eleven years. At age five, he had been with his father in the car accident that took Paul's life. Two years later, there was the fire where Maggie and Oliver lost their upstairs apartment over the flower shop that Maggie managed. She had scars from being burned as well as nightmares about the fire. But Oliver had been hit in the head by a beam in the ceiling as they escaped. He still dealt with partial amnesia.

She hoped attending camp this summer might help with his socialization skills. Two other campers had partial amnesia like Oliver. But also, importantly, no one made fun of him when he stuttered.

What Maggie wanted most was to help her son heal. He was her priority. And secondly, she wanted to help make the farm as successful as she could to support them and Gram. She owed her so much. The farm had been in financial trouble for a while, and Gram had been looking to start selling off some of the 40 acres to developers.

The flower farm was doing well, thankfully. And soon, she'd be adding the wedding venue for more added income.

Maggie took a deep breath. Focus. Work.

Sometimes she left muffins in the office for the employees who worked on the flower farm. Currently, she had close to twenty employees, some full-time, some part-time, and she appreciated every one. The peak seasons in spring and summer were the busiest. The job could be demanding with all the bending, lifting, planting and harvesting. There seemed to always be greenhouse work.

In fall and winter, she was surprised by how many people signed up for flower preservation, wreath-making and Christmas tree decoration classes.

She took down a mixing bowl and gathered up ingredients. Today, she also planned to stop in to surprise Gram. As she mixed the ingredients, she wondered about gauging interest in additional classes taught by local people.

Popping the muffins into the oven, she wondered about guest speakers as well. Maybe the woman in Portland she read about recently who specialized in the art of Japanese floral arrangement.

Sitting at the kitchen counter, she poured herself a cup of coffee, jotted down some ideas, then grabbed her clipboard. As she took the muffins out of the oven, she received a text from Zoe.

When you get this, call me ASAP!

Maggie would see Zoe in a few minutes. It was probably an issue with a vendor or someone called out sick.

Zoe, Maggie's best friend and sister-in-law, was indispensable. Her business acumen could land her a job anywhere she wanted to be. And here she was on her grandmother's farm, helping Maggie run the flower business. And now they were planning to start a wedding venue on the farm as well.

Maggie loved everything about living in Maine. From the farm, it was a thirty- to forty-minute drive south on Route One, depending on traffic, to Portland. It worked well for her business. People seemed to love to take a trip up from the city and wander around the farm.

Driving in on the gravel driveway, to the right, tucked in away from the road, one could see Gram's farmhouse, which was a rich buttercream color. A Private Residence sign was visible.

Signs directed visitors to the office of Maggie's Flower Farm and ample parking.

Walking past the office and into the farm, customers were greeted first by the big showy flowers–dahlias, peonies and sunflowers.

Multiple greenhouses in various sizes were a short walk to the left. Most of them were open to the public. People chose their items to buy and brought them back to the office either by hand or in wagons.

Beautiful fields of different flowers were visible. Early on, Maggie had set up benches for people to enjoy the view and relax.

Maggie and Oliver's house sat behind the flower fields. Far enough away so they didn't get any foot traffic. On the land behind their house, farther back on the left, stood the lavender fields.

She loved walking past the flower fields every day on her way to the office. Then turning left on the path from the office, she reached Gram's house. It only took a few minutes to walk anywhere she wanted to go. Maggie braided her thick brown hair quickly then secured it with a vintage cloisonné hair clip.

A gift from Paul, so pretty she usually only wore it on special occasions. Tying a favorite sweater around her waist, she headed out the door.

Arriving at the office, she found the door was locked. It was unlike Zoe to not be here bright and early. She liked the quiet to start her day and make any needed adjustments to the crew schedules.

Juggling the tote that held the muffins and her clipboard, Maggie unlocked the door. The bell above the door jangled, but no one called out. She left the door unlocked and half the muffins on the counter next to the schedules to be picked up by the employees.

Heading to Gram's house, she inhaled the honey-and-cloves scent of the summersweet flowers by the porch steps. Opening the screen door, she heard Zoe's laugh.

"Gram? Zoe? It's Maggie! I bring muffins!"

She walked into the living room and froze.

"Hello, Maggie. Long time, no see," said Jake.

"Umm… Hi?" Maggie's heart raced.

Zoe laughed. "Have this effect often on women, big Bro?"

"Good to see you back in Sweet Springs, Jake," Maggie said a little too brightly.

Maggie couldn't believe it. Her center of gravity shifted. Right there, sitting on Gram's yellow step stool in the living room was Jake Madison, having his thick black hair cut by his sister.

Zoe glared at her over the top of her brother's head. "Did you get my text?"

Maggie nodded.

"Why didn't you call me?" she said through clenched teeth.

"You felt you had to warn her I was home?" Jake asked dryly.

Zoe swatted his arm. Maggie noticed how strong his biceps looked beneath his T-shirt. He did not look like the Jake she remembered.

"Someone has to warn people when your ugly mug is back in town." Zoe took the cape off him and brushed his neck free of hair.

Maggie's laugh sounded like a harsh bark. To her surprise, a dog responded from his spot behind Gram's upholstered wingback chair.

"That dog!" Maggie exclaimed. "It was outside the window last night. Then it ran toward the main house."

"His name is Hero. And yes, he definitely had the zoomies when he jumped out of the tow truck. I wondered where he went."

Maggie willed her heartbeat to return to normal. Neither she nor Jake moved. They stood there staring at each other as the seconds ticked by.

Then Gram walked into the room and cleared her throat. Maggie wondered how long she'd been standing there.

"Oh how wonderful, Maggie," Gram said, "you brought muffins. C'mon everyone, let's get caught up over breakfast."

"I'll just run upstairs real quick and clean up," said Jake, breaking eye contact with Maggie. She heard him take the creaky steps two at a time.

"Are you all right?" Zoe whispered as she linked her arm with Maggie's. "I tried, girlfriend. I tried to give you a heads-up!"

"I know. Thank you. I didn't expect to see him," Maggie said.

"No one did. Apparently he wanted to surprise us," said Zoe.

Maggie drew in a deep breath.

"You watch, I bet Gram asks him a zillion questions at the table," whispered Zoe.

Minutes later, Jake joined them. "Good job on my hair, Zoe. Thank you!"

Maggie heard his stomach rumble and imagined that his sister and grandmother did as well.

"I'm starved," he said. "Let's eat!"

Zoe laughed. "Good to know some things never change."

Maggie sat opposite Zoe. Gram and Jake sat at opposite ends of the table. On the table were the muffins she'd brought, plus pancakes, bacon and eggs. A feast. She wished Oliver was here too; he'd love this.

She felt terrible for not getting up early enough to make him a proper breakfast before he left for camp today. He'd made himself a peanut butter and jelly sandwich this morning. She knew because he left the plate and knife in the sink unrinsed. Good thing the camp gave the kids lunch and snacks.

She promised herself she'd do better. Hers was an ever-growing list of *do betters*. And she would. She would keep the farm going and profitable for Gram. And she would provide a much needed income and home for her and Oliver.

Maggie stole a glance at Jake. He was still as handsome as ever. His thick black hair. Those blue eyes. That winsome smile.

She had something important to tell him before he left this time. She and Paul had come to a decision about it a long time ago. Only Zoe knew what it was.

After saying grace, there was an uncomfortable silence at the table. Gram eyed all three of them with a puzzled look on her face.

*Think about work*, Maggie told herself as she stabbed a forkful of pancakes. *Okay, what's on the agenda today?*

Right then, Gram smiled and looked at Jake. "God brought you here. So, what's your story? Inquiring minds want to know."

Maggie watched as Jake swallowed hard. She hoped he wouldn't choke.

Zoe stepped in. "Wow, Gram, grill him, why don't you?"

Everyone laughed.

"Short version for now," he said. "I was on tour as a lead guitarist in the band No Caution."

"Ah, we know that. A very successful band," Zoe chimed

in. "Jake, I'm curious. You said you were staying awhile. Don't you have to get back? Did you take a leave?"

"No job right now. I recently got back from Guatemala City. I was doing music missionary work there," Jake said.

"Wow!" exclaimed Zoe.

Jake smiled at the surprised look on his sister's face. "When I return to Kansas, I'll look for a job there. I plan to stay in the area of music ministry." He took a sip of tea.

Maggie could see beads of moisture on Jake's upper lip. He was definitely nervous about what he was about to say.

Jake continued with a hitch in his voice. "As you all know, I made some really bad decisions in the past. And I apologize for that. One of my biggest regrets was leaving you all the way I did."

Gram nodded slightly but didn't say anything.

Jake glanced at each of them in turn. "I met God again in Manhattan, Kansas. He hadn't left our relationship but I had. I realized out there after talking to a good pastor friend that I wanted to come back to see you, to try to make amends, to be part of the family again. I know it's a big ask, but I'd like the chance to try."

Following what felt like a stunned silence, Gram talked first. "I think I speak for all of us. It's good to have you home for however long you stay. Right, girls?"

Both Zoe and Maggie nodded.

Jake smiled. "Thanks. Oh, and I rescued Hero in Kansas. He's smarter than I am and knows way more commands than I do. I believe he was a support dog for a woman, but her husband didn't like big dogs."

Maggie looked at Hero sitting beside her. She fed him a piece of her pancake. She'd not known Jake to be religious. Her own relationship with God was at times questionable.

Then Jake asked, "Where's Oliver?"

"Oliver is at day camp," said Maggie.

"Day camp! Cool. The camp up by the lake?" Jake asked.

Maggie nodded. "Yes, he goes twice a week for now. See how he does."

"How he does?" asked Jake.

Zoe reached over and squeezed Maggie's hand.

"It's a camp for kids who have been through some sort of trauma. Oliver has selective amnesia and a mild stutter, which is more noticeable if he's tired or stressed."

"I'm sorry to hear you're both dealing with that, Maggie. I look forward to seeing him again."

She knew Jake was trying. "I'm not sure he'll remember you," Maggie said quietly.

"That's okay. I'm glad Gram and Zoe have been here to help you and Oliver. Count me in too. Whatever you need."

"Thank you."

"So, Jake, what kind of a beater car did you buy that didn't get you all the way here, eh?"

"Hey, Zoe, the car made it close, and Kansas is a long way from Maine, you know!" Jake said.

"How was the trip?" his sister asked.

*Good going, Zoe.* Maggie was relieved at the change of subject.

Jake leaned back. "Have I got stories!"

She caught a glimpse of the boyish grin she remembered. Jake proceeded to regale them with several tales from the trip. Mostly centered around Hero's misbehaviors, which made everyone laugh.

Zoe and Jake got up and started to clear the table.

Maggie carried a stack of plates but stopped when she overheard Jake say, "Maggie was sure thrown when she saw me. Is it because I remind her of Paul?"

Zoe gave her brother a sideways hug. Maggie waited a moment before she set the dishes on the sideboard.

"I can't stay much longer," said Zoe. "You know I've got this drill sergeant at work."

"Ha! You've never had it so good," Maggie kidded.

"Gram, I noticed the porch light blinking last night. I'll fix that today," offered Jake.

"Oh yes, I'd love it if you could take a look at it. But right now, why don't you let Maggie show you around the farm. It's a beautiful day, and she's worked so hard on it."

Jake looked at Maggie. "I'd really like that, if you have the time, Mags."

*Mags.* He was the only one who had ever called her that.

"Maybe. The dishes—"

Gram interrupted her. "Go, go. The dishes will get done sooner or later."

"I'll see you both at the office," Zoe said as she headed out. "And don't do the dishes, Gram—I'll do them when I get home later."

Maggie chewed her lip a bit and patted Hero. "Sure, Jake," she said.

She heard Jake's sigh of relief. To her surprise, he grabbed a Stetson hat from the hall tree.

Maggie smiled. "C'mon, cowboy, I'll give you the grand tour. Bring Hero too."

As they left the house, she heard Gram say loud enough for her to hear, "I wonder what the good Lord has in mind for those two."

# *Chapter Two*

Jake glanced over and saw Maggie's bright pink cheeks. She must have heard what Gram said. Could the moment be any more awkward?

"So…"

"So," Maggie said at the same time, "do you want the simple tour or the deluxe?"

Puzzled, he answered, "I'm not sure. I didn't know there would be options."

Maggie smiled. "The simple tour is what visitors see when they come to the farm."

"And the deluxe tour?" he asked.

"The deluxe tour is what I have planned for the future of the business. Either way, I should tell you, there will be coffee."

Jake thought for a minute. Then responded, "How about the simple tour today so I can get caught up with what's going on? And then I have to go to town this afternoon to buy a coffeepot for Gram and see about my car."

"Sounds good. We'll put a pin in the deluxe tour. Let's start at the office straight ahead."

"And the coffee," Jake added. "I'm definitely not forgetting that promise of coffee."

He slipped on his sunglasses. Hero caught up with them, and the three of them walked companionably down the gravel path toward the office.

As the farm came into view, it all looked familiar and yet entirely new. The days of cows grazing and farm crops were a thing of the past. There were rows of flowers, and a few wheelbarrows scattered about with plants in them. The office was a new white building with sunflowers painted on the side. A small hand-painted wooden sign, Maggie's Flower Farm, graced the front.

"This is what visitors see when they first arrive. Central headquarters for everyone working here as well."

"It was around midnight when I came in with Matt. I didn't see the sign out by the road," Jake said. He glanced up the driveway. Quite a long drive between here and the main road. He wondered if something nearer the road would be better. A big, eye-catching sign. Maybe a wooden stand that held bouquets of flowers for people to buy. Those were things he could build.

Hero stayed outside as Jake and Maggie entered the building. It was well-lit and welcoming. Jake could see a couple of desks in front and imagined more in rooms toward the back. Customers with purchases of bouquets and potted plants waited at a long counter to pay.

"I'll be right with you, Jake. Take a look around if you like," Maggie said as she headed for the cash register.

"Sure thing. Take your time." He watched her smile and greet the customers. A couple told her they were waiting for Zoe to bring in a few potted plants they'd picked out.

He walked over to a wall of framed prints for sale. Beautiful scenes of the flower fields. There were also a few large flower portraits. Others were of Maggie's team doing various jobs on the farm. One photograph featured Maggie working in a row of flowers, the morning sun just coming up over a Maine sky. He slipped it off the wall and set it on the floor. Then he chose another one, an impossibly close-up view of a peony, complete with a bumblebee.

He brought them up to the counter just as Zoe came in pulling a small blue wagon with pots of pink flowers.

Jake held up the prints. "I'd like to buy these. Can I set them behind the counter for now?"

"Absolutely!" Zoe said.

"Whose Bullmastiff is that outside?" asked a woman with a camera around her neck.

"That would be my dog. Is he behaving himself?" asked Jake.

"Yes." The woman laughed. "He's quite photogenic."

"Jake, this is our resident photographer, Molly," Zoe chimed in. "Molly, this is Jake, my older brother. He's buying some of your work."

Molly extended her hand. "Good to meet you, Jake. And I like your taste in photography," she said, giving him a broad smile.

"My pleasure to meet the photographer. How long have you been photographing Maggie's Flower Farm?" he asked.

"I met Maggie at the Sweet Springs Fair, where I had a booth. She asked if I was interested in taking some photos for her website," Molly explained.

"Ah, fortuitous," Jake said.

Molly continued, "She was my first client, and when I say that working here redefined happiness for me, I'm not exaggerating. The word of mouth from here literally started my career," Molly said with genuine warmth.

Maggie joined them. "And I have a new venture here at the farm that I hope you'll consider coming on board for as well."

"Oh! Do tell." Molly was clearly interested.

"A wedding venue here at the flower farm," said Maggie.

"I've photographed weddings and loved every minute! Count me in!" Molly said as she picked up her tripod and camera bag by the door.

"Happy to hear that! I'll be in touch," said Maggie.

Amy, the greenhouse manager, opened the office door and

called out to Zoe, "I left a wagon of plants outside the back door. A woman is coming in to pay for them."

"Good, thank you for the heads-up, Amy," Zoe replied.

Jake was happy to see the place so busy.

Maggie touched Jake's sleeve and motioned for him to follow her outside.

"What about back there?" Jake pointed to rooms off the long hall beyond the desk.

"Sorry, that's part of the deluxe tour." Maggie winked at him.

Jake was intrigued.

Zoe laughed. "You ain't seen nuthin' yet, Bro."

Jake pushed his hat back. "Lead on, Maggie," he said.

Outside she began to point out the propagation greenhouse and the hoop houses meant to extend the seasons for some of the flowers. She mentioned the names of the flowers in the rows as they passed.

Up ahead, Hero sniffed everything in sight from flowers to tools. The fawn-colored Bullmastiff seemed to love the farm. So did Maggie by the look on her face. He almost wished there was time for the deluxe tour today.

Jake had so many questions he wanted to ask her. All of them too personal this soon or maybe ever. He'd start with something connected to the farm. "Can I ask you something?"

"Sure," Maggie said. She blew upward at a stray hair dangling over her face.

"Why flowers? How did you come to run a flower farm?"

Maggie stopped walking, "Well," she hesitated, looking up at him. "You know I ran a florist shop for years in North Carolina?"

Jake nodded.

She started walking again. He noticed she subconsciously rubbed a scar on her arm. She continued, "After the fire, I found working with the flowers comforting, healing. The variety of colors and scents. Their beauty made me happy."

He watched Maggie's face soften. "I began fantasizing about what it would be like to be on the other side of the business. To do more than just sell them. I began reading books and sketching out plans. It all seemed like a fantasy."

Jake wanted to know more. "Yes, it seems like quite a leap from that to this," he said.

Maggie smiled. "It's all happening because of a phone call from Gram suggesting Oliver and I move here after the fire."

Jake felt a pang of guilt. He should have called her too, but he was too wrapped up in his grief and regret over his brother Paul.

Maggie put her hands in her pockets. "Paul and I moved a lot. It felt like we never really settled down. I'm happy to say this finally feels like home."

All of this spoke volumes to Jake. Had Paul and Maggie been happy?

He remembered that she'd grown up in foster care, and wondered if that played into her decision to move as well. No doubt giving Oliver family would be a priority for her.

Maggie circled back. "You asked, why flowers? I've always felt in tune with them. Flowers are rooted, they need nutrients, water, sunshine like we do. Yet they are tenacious, seeds blow in the wind and take root wherever they land. I can understand flowers. The rest of life not so much. Flowers, yes."

"But this farm is different from selling flowers. How did you build the business up like this?" Jake asked.

Maggie smiled. "I tapped everyone I knew. Flower people are wonderful about wanting to help. At least, it's been my experience here in the East. I joined the Association of Specialty Cut Flowers."

"It's really all quite impressive, Mags," Jake said.

"Thank you. I read…a lot. I followed crumbs of ideas and went down rabbit holes of research. I visited as many of the flower farms in Maine as I could. Zoe went with me. Afterward, we sat in the car and wrote notes of what we'd learned.

Our location is good. We're not a long drive from Portland. A lot of trial and error. And *voila*," she said, sweeping her arms, "here we are now."

Jake was in awe of all she'd accomplished.

An uncomfortable silence followed. He wondered if she worried she'd shared too much with him.

Given their past history together and his abrupt departure, she had good reason to be guarded. He deserved it, but it still didn't make it any easier.

"Maybe we should head back so you can get to town for your errands," Maggie suggested. She felt drained after the short tour. She definitely needed a break.

She watched the workers moving through the fields. Her focus needed to be on the workday ahead. She made a mental note to check the hoop houses later.

"Maggie," someone called from the row of flowers they were approaching. "A customer has a question."

"Be right there," she called out. "This shouldn't take long. I'll catch up with you."

She quickly answered the person's flower questions. Then she spied Jake strolling with Hero up ahead. They were clearly bonded. The Bullmastiff nudged Jake's hand for attention, which he readily gave.

She noted Jake walked with a swagger now. He'd always had a certain charisma. It was no wonder he'd become such a success in country music.

Almost catching up to them, she studied Jake. He seemed quiet, deep in thought. In the past, she'd always gotten lost gazing into his blue eyes, but they weren't visible with his sunglasses. His black hair peeked out from under the Stetson.

There was softness in his features in the morning light. Smoothed out edges from the rougher version of the man she'd seen in music videos and on the pages of tabloids. Also quite different from the grief-stricken man who'd attended Paul's funeral. And he'd never been particularly religious before. The changes were surprising, but she also found them intriguing.

She wondered about his time in Kansas. There were so many questions she wanted to ask him. But would she? She wasn't as heartbroken now, but she still felt hurt from when he'd left her behind years ago. Jake hadn't cared to share anything about his life with her or Paul over the years. That was what hurt the most.

Maggie didn't know who he was now. But she knew one thing for certain: he'd be leaving for Kansas soon.

Maybe they would share good memories of Paul on this visit. It could be healing for them both. She needed to decide when and if she'd upend Jake's world with what she and Paul had always been planning to tell him. Her stomach flipped at the thought of it.

"Mission accomplished with the customer?" Jake asked as she caught up to him.

Maggie nodded. They still walked back to the office, and she couldn't help herself. "Can I ask *you* something now?"

"Sure thing," he said.

"Why are you here? Why now, Jake?" It came out a bit harsher than she intended.

His raised eyebrows told her that he picked up on her tone.

"No ulterior motives, I promise you. It's like I said this morning, I'm here to make amends for the stupid way I've handled some things in my life and move on. That and I'm here because I've missed my family."

Despite everything, she believed him. "I didn't mean to put you on the defensive, Jake. It's just been a long time..."

"It has been. It's okay, Mags. No worries."

She heard his words, but his fleeting, tight smile told her otherwise.

When they finally arrived back at the office, Maggie was

grateful for Gram's visit after her daily walk. It allowed her a moment to calm her edgy nerves.

Everyone headed into the office as Maggie checked her watch. Oliver would be home soon. She almost wished she could get Jake to head into town before Oliver arrived. But she couldn't keep them apart for all of Jake's visit. Plus, it wasn't like he'd take one look at Oliver and... *Don't go there,* she told herself.

She almost let out a sigh of relief when Jake said that he should get going. He thanked Maggie for the tour and told her that he looked forward to seeing more of the farm.

"Good luck with your car," Zoe called out from the counter.

Maggie began looking out the window for Oliver. And soon enough, there he was walking up the drive with his head down. It seemed like he didn't have a good day. Then she saw Jake standing beside his car looking at Oliver.

She and Gram walked out together to greet her son. Out of nowhere, Hero came running. Perhaps Jake had called him to go to town with him.

Hero ran up to Gram to be petted, his tongue lolling to one side.

Maggie saw Oliver's mood brighten as he started running toward them. "G.G., you got a d-d-dog?"

Gram answered, "No, honey. This isn't my dog, but he'll be visiting us for a little while."

"That's s-super," said Oliver. He reached out tentatively to pat Hero, who immediately sat down in front of him. Oliver knelt on the ground and threw his arms around the dog's neck.

Maggie was amazed at how much her son liked the dog. She didn't even know he liked dogs. He had never even mentioned wanting one. Had Paul liked dogs? She didn't remember. It would have been difficult to have a dog in the apartment above the flower shop back in North Carolina.

"Who does he belong to?" Oliver asked as Hero slurped him on the cheek.

"That would be me," said Jake.

"He's a w-w-wonderful dog," Oliver said.

"That he is," Jake agreed.

Jake looked at Maggie and she nodded.

"Oliver, I'm your Uncle Jake. Your father's brother. I don't know if you remember me?" he said gently.

Oliver's blue eyes widened. He stood up, hugged himself tightly and took a step back.

Maggie scrambled to remember when the last time Jake saw Oliver was. At Paul's funeral? Maggie just looked at her anxious son as he silently stared at Jake.

Jake's expression seemed pained. She could see how much Jake wanted to hug Oliver. She was grateful he was holding himself back.

"It's all right if you don't remember me," Jake said. "We can get to know each other again while I'm here. And I think Hero wants to get to know you too." Hero wagged his tail and looked from Jake to Oliver.

Maggie put a hand on Oliver's back. "Are you ókay, honey? Do you not feel well?"

Oliver looked at her. "Is—is—is he mad at me?" Oliver's voice trembled. "Is he—he—he here because he's m-m-mad at me?"

"What? No honey. Jake isn't mad at you—are you, Jake?" Maggie looked at Jake, her eyes wide. She shrugged her shoulders.

"No, I'm not mad at all, buddy," Jake said. "Really! I'm just glad to see you."

His puzzled expression probably matched her own right now.

Jake turned slowly toward Maggie. "Okay, folks, I've gotta run to town. Maybe Hero could stay here at the farm so he can get to know Oliver?"

Gram chimed in, "Isn't that nice? I think we'd all like that. What do you think, Oliver?"

Oliver scuffed his shoe on the gravel and nodded. He kept his eyes on Hero, who leaned against him.

"Okay then, I'll be going," said Jake, looking at Gram then Maggie. He looked at Oliver longingly.

Gram handed Jake the keys to her truck. "Have a safe trip. Hope there's good news on your car. Love you," she said, patting his arm.

"Bye, Jake," said Maggie with a catch in her voice.

"Hero, stay," said Jake as he turned to go. "Thank you again for the loan of the pickup, Gram."

"See you soon, Oliver," Jake said over his shoulder. As he walked away she wondered if he thought not approaching him with a face-to-face goodbye would be less stress for Oliver.

Maggie saw Oliver visibly shudder.

Maggie had no idea why and wanted to find out the reason as soon as possible. Right now, she didn't want Oliver out of her sight. And it looked like Hero felt the same way.

# *Chapter Three*

Jake kept replaying the scene over and over again.

He had no idea what just happened. It wasn't so much Oliver not remembering him—that he could accept. But why would Oliver think he was mad at him?

There was no way he was leaving Sweet Springs until he got to the bottom of this. That boy was his nephew. His family.

Jake could see a lot of himself in Oliver. Which was only natural. After all, Paul was his brother.

When Jake pulled into Matt Cyr's garage, he saw his Toyota parked in one of the bays. It was a busy place. He was genuinely happy for what Matt had accomplished. Jake honked and parked around the side of the building.

"Hey, Jake, I see your grandmother lent you her truck," Matt said, wiping his hands on a rag.

Jake looked back at the pickup. "I have a feeling you've pulled off some fancy mechanics keeping Gram's pickup going. It's seen plenty of miles. Still a sweet ride though."

"Wish I could say I can do the same for your car," Matt laughed.

"C'mon Matt, say it ain't so!"

"No, Jake," Matt said. "Seriously, it has some issues, but they can be fixed. Your alternator is shot. The head gasket is leaking. And the exhaust pipes are rusted out from the manifold back. And…"

"Just fix it all, Matt. I don't know whether to sell it or keep it to drive back to Kansas, but I sure can't do anything with it in the shape it's in." Jake shook his head.

"I'll replace the alternator first," Matt suggested.

"Sounds good, I guess. I need to get my stuff out of it. Let me go grab some boxes from the back of the pickup. Be right back."

"Yeah, I saw your guitar there. I knew you wanted to take it the other night, but there wasn't room for a harmonica with you, me and that huge dog in the truck cab," Matt said.

Jake laughed. "Thanks, Matt, I really appreciate your keeping my guitar safe." That guitar wasn't the one he played onstage. It was one he had bought for himself before his success. It was the trusted friend that had helped him write every one of his songs. It was the guitar that Pastor Joe saw him sleeping next to in the church pew on that morning that changed his life.

He loaded up his suitcases. A couple boxes of books. His leather case of extra guitar strings, picks and a tuner. Hero's toys included his favorite squeaky purple pineapple, which Jake was sure the dog was looking for. He saw him nosing Jake's backpack once or twice. Finally, he lugged everything back to the truck.

Matt came around the corner with his guitar. "All set, Jake? Someone here wants to see you before you leave."

Jake's stomach flip-flopped. He didn't know if he was ready to meet and greet. He still hated answering questions about his past.

"Yeah, who?" he asked casually as he put the guitar in the cab.

"An old buddy of ours from high school. Kevin Tibbets. Remember him?"

"Sure. I'll come say hi in just a sec." Jake remembered Kevin. He'd been girl crazy back then. Maybe he'd settled down by now. He tossed his Stetson on the seat.

Jake turned around to see Kevin coming at him, hand outstretched.

"Hey, Jake! Good to see you! The hometown boy who made good!" Kevin grabbed Jake's hand and shook it like he was trying to pump water out of a well.

"Hi, Kevin." Jake extracted what was left of his hand. He resisted the urge to massage it. "How've you been?"

"Can't complain. I run Tibbet's Sporting Goods now. Took over the family business. Anything you need, stop by."

"Thanks. Don't know how long I'll be around."

"So, Jake, heard you left the band. I don't know how you could do it." Kevin winked at him.

"It's a long story, but it was for the best."

"Sure, sure… I should stop by the farm and see you some time. Haven't been out there since I dated your sister. Zoe still doing trick riding?"

"Of course!" Jake had no idea if she was or wasn't. He knew next to nothing about his sister's life right now.

"Well, I better get going now. See you around, dude," Kevin said.

"Yeah," said Jake. "Sure thing." He shook his head as he watched Kevin leave.

Matt stepped out of the garage. "Kevin gone already?"

Jake nodded. "Yeah, and thank you for the news on the car, I think," he said with a grin.

"Good having you back, man. I'll be in touch," said Matt.

In the cab, he called Gram.

"I'm going to drive around town, see what's new. Maybe stop at the Wild Onion Diner. Anything you need?" he asked.

"Not that I can think of. Have fun, Jake. See you when you get back."

Jake turned into the parking lot of Old Grace Church. He always thought of it as Gram's church. Soon he'd be attending Sunday services with her again. Right now though, he needed to collect his thoughts. The front doors were wide open. But there were no cars around. He wandered in quietly. A man cleaning the church pews nodded at him, and he nodded back.

Taking a seat, he closed his eyes and prayed for guidance. For blessings for his family. And for help making amends with them. Regrets tightened his chest.

Oliver came to mind. The way he'd walked up the driveway with his head down tugged at Jake's heartstrings. He asked God for a way to help him. Oliver had seemed to bond with Hero. Maybe that was the way in.

He prayed some more then headed back out to Gram's truck, nicknamed Bessie. Getting in, he thought about how much Hero would love riding on the bench seat with his head out the window.

His stomach grumbled. Next stop: Wild Onion Diner.

Pulling in, the place looked just the same. A spruced-up old railroad car. He, Paul and Zoe would beg to sit at the counter a few minutes while their parents sat at a booth before their orders arrived. The kids loved it when they twirled on the red stools, their feet not reaching the floor. It always made the customers and staff smile.

A moment later, he couldn't believe his eyes. There was Maggie getting out of a Subaru.

He waved and saw her eyes widen. She didn't frown, so that was a good sign.

"Jake what are you doing here?" she asked.

"Having lunch. Care to join me?"

"I was just stopping in for a frappe. I'm meeting a potential customer in an hour. Sure, why not," Maggie said.

They walked in and slid into a red vinyl upholstered booth. The food smelled so good, Jake wanted one of everything.

The former owner's daughter, Riley? No… Ruby zeroed in on them.

"Jake! Is that you? Good to see you, Maggie. You bring that

sweet son of yours in sometime. I always have some apple pie with his name on it."

"Will do," said Maggie.

"Jake, it's powerful good to see you here. We've all missed you. 'Course we saw you on TV or in *People* magazine from time to time." Ruby bent down and gave Jake a hug, which surprised him. Pleasantly so.

"Ruby, you haven't changed a bit. And the place is as busy as ever! Is your mom still here?" Jake asked.

"No, sadly, she passed away a few years ago, but I run it now and love it. Every day is different. And I get to feed people. What will you two have? I recommend today's meatloaf. And there's some homemade peach pie." Ruby pulled out her pen and order book.

"Sorry to hear about your mother, Ruby," Jake said.

Ruby nodded. The look on her face indicated she still missed her.

"What I want is a Wild Onion burger. Do you still make those?" Jake asked hopefully.

"With homemade fried onions, bacon and yellow banana peppers?"

"Oh yes, please!" said Jake enthusiastically.

"Maggie?" asked Ruby

"Just a mocha frappe for me," she answered.

"You got it. How about some sweet potato fries to share? No one can resist Wild Onion's sweet potato fries," Ruby said.

Jake smiled. "Yes, all of it. Hurry!"

"Oh honey, I missed you!" Ruby stuck her pen behind her ear and chuckled all the way to the back.

Jake heard her call out, "Frank, extra-special order."

"Do you remember when we'd come here after the football games and it was so crowded and loud, we couldn't hear ourselves think?" he asked.

"I do remember," said Maggie.

"Then we'd go walk around the town picking out things we wanted from store windows." Jake sat back and looked at Maggie. It wasn't hard to picture how she'd looked years ago sitting in probably this same booth.

To Jake's regret, there wasn't more time for trips down memory lane before the food arrived.

After the last fry was eaten and the last drop of milkshake gone, Maggie headed to the counter with Jake.

"Same check?" asked Ruby.

"No," said Maggie at the same time Jake said, "Yes."

"I'm happy to pay, Maggie," Jake said.

"Thank you, Jake, but that's not necessary," she said as she opened her wallet.

Jake stepped back to let her pay. Maggie called out to thank Ruby and told Jake she'd see him later, she had to go.

Jake caught a whiff of the pretty flower arrangement that was standing near the cash register. It reminded him of Maggie.

Ruby came up and touched his arm. "Take this peach pie home to the family. Compliments of the house." She handed him a pie all boxed up.

"Ruby..."

"Think of it as a homecoming present, Jake."

Jake lifted the pie up to smell it. "Mmmm, thank you, Ruby," he said.

"And I'll see you out at the farm. Every week I drive out to get some bouquets made up for the diner, like this one. The customers love them."

"I think the cooking and the owner have something to do with that too," Jake said.

Ruby added, "And of course, I get to visit Maggie. It was real good seeing her today."

"Agreed," he said as he returned another heartfelt hug from Ruby. Then he headed carefully outside with his precious cargo that would ride home next to his guitar and Stetson.

* * *

It was hard not to think about the past after eating lunch with Jake at the Wild Onion Diner. To her credit she didn't give in to the temptation to keep reminiscing. Though she certainly wanted to.

Heading into the kitchen, she watched Oliver as he poked around in the refrigerator. After finding an apple, he closed the fridge and washed it in the sink. No doubt he'd go watch TV or play games on his computer in his room. So far, he was good about the screen time rules she'd set in place. She hoped it would always be that way, she thought, but doubted it would be.

Maggie didn't want to be a helicopter mom, but she was so worried about him. He was a bit better about opening up lately. She was loath to push him. But what happened earlier with Jake replayed in her mind.

There was no way that Oliver could know Paul was not his father.

She knew that didn't mean that it was all right to keep the truth from Jake any longer. She and Paul had decided to tell him when the time was right. Jake was here now.

The knock at the door startled Maggie.

"I'll g-get it, M-Mom," Oliver called out.

She held her breath, worried that Jake would show up.

Then she heard Zoe's laughter. Maggie was surprised to see her laden down with containers of food. Maggie was grateful that Zoe never spoke loudly to Oliver as if he had hearing problems as well as his shyness and stutter. Some people did, and she always cringed when the conversation became very stilted or Oliver shut down. She remembered Jake was normal with him earlier, as well.

"What's all this?" asked Maggie, delighted with the smells filling the kitchen.

"You know Gram. She really doesn't know how to cook for

less than ten people." Zoe laughed. "Oliver, can you help?" Zoe leaned down so he could take the plastic container on top.

Maggie smiled as she saw Oliver eyeing the food.

Heading to the kitchen, Maggie said, "This is wonderful! Stay with us and have some?" She started spreading out the containers and peeking at what was inside.

"Hoped you might ask," Zoe grinned. "I told those two I might visit awhile. Let me give them a quick call." She pulled out her cell phone. "It'll give them a chance to get caught up too."

"Did Hero come with you?" Oliver asked Zoe.

"No, honey, but if you two walk me home later, I'm sure you will see him then."

Oliver nodded enthusiastically. He went to the cupboard for plates then pulled out silverware from the drawer. Maggie knew he wanted to eat as quickly as possible.

"I think someone is suddenly a dog lover," Maggie said while uncovering the containers and casserole dishes.

"I think you might be right," Zoe agreed.

Maggie inhaled deeply. *Lasagna!* There were also two different salads and garlic breadsticks.

As Oliver reached for a breadstick, the phone rang. Zoe held up a finger that she'd be just a moment. She mouthed "business" as she answered her phone. Maggie smiled when Oliver closed his eyes as he chewed.

"Problems tomorrow with coverage?" Maggie asked when Zoe returned.

"No, the vendor wanted to know if we can make a delivery earlier than scheduled. Already dealt with it, we can do it," Zoe said.

"You're a marvel, you truly are. Thank you!" Maggie said appreciatively.

Maggie filled three glasses and the water pitcher. Then she

sat down with the two of them. After they said grace, she took a deep breath and her stomach growled. Laughter filled the room.

"Guess I got here with food just in time!" Zoe said.

Zoe took some tossed green salad.

Then she turned to Oliver. "So, what do you think of your Uncle Jake?"

Maggie choked on the salad dressing and started coughing. Zoe hadn't seen how Oliver reacted to Jake earlier.

"S'okay," he said with his head down as if concentrating intently on the food on his plate. Which might very well be the case, Maggie thought as she tried to catch Zoe's attention.

"He was a country rock star years ago, you know," said Zoe as she spooned some cranberry salad on her plate.

Oliver looked at her. "R-r-really? Wow, y-y-you should have t-t-told me, Mom!"

"That's right. He was part of the rock band No Caution," said Zoe.

Maggie bumped her toe into Zoe's shin.

"Ow!" Zoe looked at Maggie, clearly clueless.

Oliver quickly scarfed down his food. "I—I—I know them. M-M-Mom has all their m-m-music."

"Does she now?" Zoe teased Maggie.

"Well, we would, wouldn't we? Jake being family and all," declared Maggie.

Oliver asked to be excused. It was Tuesday night, and Oliver's favorite musical talent show was on. Sometimes they watched it together.

Tonight though, she knew Zoe wanted to talk.

"Enjoy the show!" she told her son.

Quietly, she and Zoe cleared away the dishes, rinsed them off and put them into the dishwasher.

"Want to sit on the porch?" Zoe suggested.

Maggie nodded and shut the window in the kitchen in case Oliver went in for a snack. He knew there were still pieces of a peach pie that Gram sent over. Zoe had mentioned that Jake brought it back from town earlier.

She settled in a comfy chair on the porch.

Zoe got straight to the point. "Are you thinking about telling Jake about Oliver?"

The subject was full of so many conflicting emotions. "You know Paul and I always planned to tell Jake together, then Gram."

"You don't think Gram knows?" asked Zoe.

"I haven't told her. Paul would have told me if he did. You didn't tell her, did you?"

"Of course not," said Zoe emphatically. "I'll stand in for Paul if you need me to. You know that, right?"

Tears welled up in Maggie's eyes. She shook her head. "You're wonderful to offer, but no, I'll tell Jake alone. Then we can decide about telling Gram."

Zoe nodded. "She won't be happy about not knowing."

"The thing is, Jake and Gram can know. But I don't want Oliver to know yet. I don't know how Jake will react," Maggie said.

"I'm betting they'll both understand," Zoe said. "Jake did see how Oliver is, earlier? How quiet he is?"

"Yeah. It didn't go well," Maggie said, nervously fidgeting.

"What happened? They didn't like each other? Or what?" Zoe asked in disbelief.

Maggie's chest ached as she filled her in.

"And you have no idea what he meant by that? Why on earth would he think his uncle was mad at him?" Zoe reached out and squeezed Maggie's hand.

"I was completely blindsided, as were Jake and Gram. But Oliver hasn't mentioned anything since and doesn't seem to be dwelling on it." Maggie still felt blindsided. She could only imagine how Jake felt.

"It's baffling, all right," said Zoe. "Are you going to talk to him about it tonight?"

"I doubt I'll bring it up tonight. You saw how he was at dinner. He was interested in Jake being a musician. He didn't shut down when his name was mentioned. I just don't get it." Maggie squeezed the bridge of her nose.

"I guess you could see how they interact when they're together again," suggested Zoe.

Maggie nodded. "It's like a tsunami building. Everything is happening at once."

Zoe gulped. "You know I'm here if you need me."

Oliver's TV show ended, and he came out onto the porch. His brown hair was tousled from lying on the couch.

"Okay, gang," Zoe said as she stood up. "Want to walk me home?"

Oliver nodded. "I get to see Hero," he said.

"And you," she said, pointing at Maggie, "can explain to Gram why her dishes aren't clean and coming back with us."

"That's all right, I'll tell her that you talked our ears off and we couldn't get anything done," Maggie said as she picked up one of the comfy pillows she brought out and threw it at Zoe. Then she lightly tossed another one at Oliver who stood there stunned for a moment. Then he and Zoe laughed as they both threw them right back at Maggie.

It did Maggie's heart good to hear everyone's laughter.

As they walked back to Gram's, Hero came running over to greet them. Again, Oliver acted like the world revolved around Jake's dog. It continued to amaze Maggie.

As they neared the main house, Jake stepped out on the porch. He looked relaxed in the moonlight as he leaned on the porch railing. "Hi. Hero heard your voice, Oliver. He wanted to be let out to come find you."

Oliver looked at Hero in amazement and gave the dog another big hug.

Maggie thought Jake was trying hard to bond with Oliver. Perhaps Hero could help with that.

"I'm heading in," Zoe said. "Thank you for inviting me tonight, you two."

"You brought the food!" said Maggie.

"Tell them I said hello," Gram called out from inside. "Heading to bed."

It was a starry night with only a few clouds. The moonflowers were in full bloom on their trellises. Maggie closed her eyes and inhaled their sweet scent. Nearby, Oliver ran around in circles with Hero.

She was caught by surprise at the intensity of Jake's gaze when she opened her eyes.

"When do you think you can fit me in for the deluxe tour?"

Her heartbeat accelerated a bit. "How about tomorrow? After nine? Oliver catches the bus to camp by then."

"Sounds good to me. You know I'm willing to help on the farm anytime too," Jake offered.

Maggie smiled. "Careful, I may take you up on that. There's always plenty of work to be done."

Jake walked down the stairs. "How about I walk you both back home?"

"Sure, if you want to," she said.

On the way back, Maggie mentioned the upcoming Summer Celebration in Sweet Springs. Jake seemed evasive and didn't say whether or not he was going. Mostly they walked in silence as they watched Hero and Oliver running up ahead. She couldn't help but hope that Oliver would sleep well tonight after being all tuckered out.

"Did you learn any more about why Oliver said what he did earlier?" Jake whispered just before they reached her home.

Maggie shook her head.

"It's all right, Mags. I'm a patient man. I'll go slowly with him. As long as it takes. He's family."

For a man who had gone as far away as he could from family, he was certainly doing the opposite now. And he wanted to build a relationship with Oliver.

Maggie's breath hitched. "Jake, there's something I need to talk to you about…tomorrow."

"Okay, Mags." Jake arched his eyebrows. "We can talk when you give me that deluxe tour of the farm. See you tomorrow." He whistled for Hero, which brought Oliver to them as well.

At the door, Oliver's good-night wishes included both Hero and Uncle Jake. Jake had a smile on his face as he turned to go.

Maggie knew it was finally time to tell him the truth. Tomorrow.

# *Chapter Four*

Maggie was up before the birds.

She was glad the second floor was a new addition to their house. The floors didn't creak as she paced and wouldn't wake Oliver.

In another hour or so, she'd go downstairs and make blueberry pancakes and bacon for breakfast. Something special. With the lack of sleep, she'd have to make coffee before those pancakes.

Instead, she picked up her work binder.

Her schedule was open today. Except for taking Jake around the farm again. But that wasn't what was keeping her on edge. She also planned to tell him about Oliver. Her stomach flipped at the mere thought of it.

Without a doubt, she needed him to understand that they couldn't tell Oliver. Not yet.

Maggie and Paul had thought of so many ways to begin this long overdue conversation. She'd practiced what she'd say all night, both awake and asleep. Now everything was all jumbled in her head.

A few hours later, heading toward the farm office to meet Jake, she checked the weather again on her phone. Forecasters predicted sunshine now with rain coming in later in the day. There would be humidity and mosquitoes galore this afternoon. Hopefully most of the weeding would be finished by then.

When she got close, Maggie saw Jake helping Mrs. Baschem, one of her steady customers, with her weekly wagonful of flowers. He nodded to her, before they disappeared around the corner.

She waved to Jake as she headed into the office and asked where Zoe was.

"As far as I know, she's outside by the greenhouse," said Gloria, a greenhouse worker who was just coming into the office. "We just finished cutting the flowers for the Pelletier wedding, and I heard her get a phone call. It sounded urgent."

"Okay." Maggie waved. "Thanks, Gloria."

She almost bumped into Jake coming in as she headed out. "Ready for the deluxe tour when you are," he said.

"Just a sec. There may be some emergency. I need to talk to Zoe." Maggie grabbed a pair of work gloves from a hook by the door.

Maggie saw the concern on Jake's face. "Is she all right? What happened?"

"I think it's a flower emergency. Zoe is fine as far as I know." They both saw Zoe heading their way, throwing her hands up in the air as she got closer.

"Doesn't look like good news," Jake said.

*No, it doesn't*, Maggie thought. She hoped the order wasn't cancelled.

Zoe beckoned them inside.

"It's the Pelletier wedding in Woodstone. The refrigerated truck they were going to use to pick up the flowers is broken. No refrigeration. They can't come get the flowers. They offered to pay double or name a price if we can get them there in time. We don't have to set up—they have that covered. I told them we'd call them right back. I know things happen but..." Zoe stood there, hands on hips, her expression saying it all.

Maggie thought a moment. "We have our truck here today. We might be able to do it. Though it's quite a drive west from here. Okay, get them on the phone for me, please." Maggie chewed the inside of her cheek and picked up the work schedule on Zoe's desk.

Zoe handed Maggie her phone, and she worked out the details with the bride's mother. Zoe quickly radioed for help in loading the flowers.

"Who's going to drive there? Do you want me to go?" Zoe asked.

"No, I'd rather you stayed here," Maggie said, trying to figure things out. "I'll drive. Who can I get to go with me?"

Maggie's thoughts were racing a mile a minute.

"Me?" suggested Jake.

"You?" Maggie and Zoe said in unison.

"Me." Jake grinned. "I can help with the delivery, the driving, whatever you need."

Two of the greenhouse workers, Troy and Gloria, arrived. "I'll pull the truck around back," Gloria said to Maggie. "We can load everything in the shade."

There were twenty buckets of flowers. The floral centerpieces would have to be safely secured for the trip. The ventilated boxes for the floral bridal attire were ready. The bridal bouquet for this wedding was huge and had a larger box of its own.

Maggie nodded to them.

"Thank you, Jake. I actually think I'll take you up on that offer," said Maggie. Turning to Zoe, she suggested, "If you need more help here, maybe you could call someone in?"

Zoe laughed. "It'll be fine. You two just drive safe. It's quite a drive out there to Woodstone. It's at least forty minutes north and that's depending on traffic. You'll be cutting it close as it is because they'll still need to set things up for the wedding."

"That's true. Hope we don't hit any traffic on the way. I'll grab what we need." Zoe waved her over.

"I know you were thinking of having the talk with Jake sooner rather than later," Zoe said softly.

"It'll be fine." Maggie rubbed the scar on her forearm; it was feeling achy today. She thanked Zoe and told her to call in lunch for the crew today.

"Will do, boss. Safe trip. Take care of her, big Bro," Zoe said as she wagged a finger at her brother.

"Will do. Just here to help the boss lady," Jake said with a grin.

Maggie noticed him checking out her arm stretches. "You better stretch your muscles too, mister. You'll be using them today."

"Me?" Jake humphed. "I'm in good shape. Don't you worry about me."

Sitting so close to Jake in the cab of the truck, Maggie found it difficult to relax and enjoy the scenery.

Jake noticed Maggie rubbing her arm earlier. He wasn't thrilled that she insisted on driving the refrigerated truck, but he knew it was for the best. Time was tight. Even though they'd programmed the route in the GPS, she knew the roads better than he did.

"Do things like this happen often?" he asked. He noticed her determined yet anxious profile as she kept checking the time on the truck dashboard.

"Not like this. Though there's always something happening at the farm. Never a dull moment." He watched Maggie as she checked the mirrors to change lanes. "And I wouldn't have it any other way."

She handled the large truck like a pro. In fact, he was quite impressed at how she was handling the whole situation. He admired the way she took charge and her decision-making skills. Both Maggie and his sister had worked like a well-oiled machine to solve the problem.

Jake was amazed at all those buckets of flowers and assorted boxes that had been loaded. He couldn't help but wonder how much money the farm would have lost if they couldn't deliver them.

"You're staring at me, Jake," Maggie said.

"Sorry, Mags, I was thinking how well you handled everything back there."

"Well, thank you," she said. Then, in an obvious effort to change the subject, she asked him to tell her something about Kansas.

He drew in a deep breath. "The sky and the landscape are wide open, vast. So few trees compared to Maine. In Kansas, the sun can be relentless. Let's face it, a baseball cap like I'm wearing today doesn't cut it out west."

"I'll need to remember to wear mine once we get to the venue. The sun is quite bright today. I try to protect my skin and eyes in the Maine sun." Maggie checked the rearview mirror to see who was coming behind her and signaled a lane change.

Jake reached down between the seats. He set her cap atop her bag and then continued, "And it's illegal to hunt whales."

"Whaaat?" Maggie chuckled. "Now you're just messing with me."

"No really, it's true. A real law. It's also illegal to put ice cream on cherry pie," he said.

Maggie shook her head. "Well, in Maine, it's illegal to blow one's nose in Waterville, but that's about the only weird law I know of. Kansas sounds, um, interesting."

Jake laughed. He'd never thought of a state having its own personality.

He didn't want to, but he closed his eyes; just for a minute, he told himself. After snoozing for a short while, Jake woke up when the truck slowed and drove up a long gravel driveway. The Pelletier wedding was being held on what looked like an estate.

"Sorry for the nap," he said sheepishly to Maggie.

"No problem, I take it as a compliment. You trust my driving." Maggie maneuvered the truck around the side of the building, where she was asked to bring the flowers.

They were met by an older gentleman in formal attire. Maggie had hoped a crew would be there to help unload.

"Hello. I'm Jeffrey, the wedding planner." He spoke into the mic on his headset, telling someone that the flowers had arrived. Two young people arrived to help with the unloading. They stood shoulder to shoulder as Jake opened the back of the truck.

Maggie explained to Jeffrey what flowers were in each bucket. Consulting his clipboard, he directed his people where they should be taken. As for the trays of corsages and boutonnieres, he told a young woman to quickly take them upstairs.

Suddenly, Mrs. Pelletier appeared. "Well done, Jeffrey," she said. He nodded and took his leave.

"I'm so happy you could do this. Can you imagine my daughter's wedding without flowers? You arrived with just enough time to spare." Mrs. Pelletier fanned herself even though it wasn't that warm out.

"It was our pleasure. I'm so glad we were able to help make the wedding a success." Maggie added, "It's a lovely day for a wedding."

"Yes, why don't you and your helper stay for the wedding," Mrs. Pelletier offered graciously.

"Thank you but no, we really aren't dressed properly," said Maggie.

Jake looked at a few well-dressed guests milling about the grounds and had to agree.

"However, I'd love to peek at the wedding setup, if that's all right?" Maggie added.

"Of course, you may. Enjoy yourselves. I must be off, but I'll be in touch soon. I think our negotiation on the price earlier was too low," Mrs. Pelletier said before she left them standing there.

"Should we move the truck if we're staying?" Jake asked.

"We're not blocking an entryway, and we'll only be a few minutes," Maggie whispered, as if they were doing something they hadn't asked permission for.

"I have to say, I'm surprised that you don't want to stay for the wedding but you want to see what it all looks like?" Jake tilted his head as if it really didn't make sense to him.

Standing in front of her, he looked into her glistening green eyes.

"This," she said slowly, "is my dream. I plan to host weddings at the farm. I want to do indoor receptions in the barn. And outdoor weddings, perhaps in a gazebo we'll build." Her smile took his breath away. It reminded him of a younger Maggie.

"I think it's a good idea if you can pull it off." Most likely he wouldn't be around by the time it became a reality. But that didn't mean he couldn't help out in the meantime.

"Let's go, quick, before more guests arrive." Maggie ran around the truck toward the wedding venue.

Standing near the edge of the dining area, he watched her absorbing it all. There was so much hustle and bustle. He moved several times to get out of the way. But not Maggie. She stood there mesmerized.

"C'mon," she whispered, "I want to see where the wedding ceremony will be taking place."

Jake followed her as she wove through waiters carrying trays. Suddenly, she stopped and stared at an archway of flowers. The first chair in each aisle held a small vase that was being filled with Maggie's flowers.

He heard Maggie gasp.

"Magical. That's the very arch I've imagined." Her mouth curved into a smile.

At that moment, Jake wanted to do whatever it took to make it a reality to have weddings like this at the farm.

"We can go now," she said wistfully as she headed back to the truck.

"Are you sure? We could stay a while longer," Jake offered.

"No, we should get back to the farm. I'm sorry you didn't get the deluxe tour today," Maggie said.

"Ah, but Mags, this was part of the deluxe tour."

She looked at him. "How so?"

"Didn't you tell me that the deluxe tour is what's there and what you have planned for the farm?" Jake took off his baseball cap and combed his fingers through his hair. "You shared some of your hopes and dreams for the farm today."

The earlier unflappable Maggie gave him a weary smile. "How about the planned deluxe tour at the farm tomorrow then?" she asked.

Jake nodded.

Maggie yawned twice and almost staggered as they walked back to the truck. "How about letting me drive back, Mags?" he said.

She didn't say a word as she fished the keys out of her pocket.

A moment later, Jake looked down at the keys she'd just placed in his palm. He knew this was a lot for Maggie as she preferred to be in control. She trusted him to drive the refrigerated truck that was vitally important for her business.

That made him smile.

# *Chapter Five*

The next day, Jake recalled how he and Maggie had sung along to several songs on the oldies station on the way back to the farm. When they'd stopped singing, he'd noticed that she'd tried hard not to fall asleep in the truck

He wondered how hard she drove herself. As soon as they returned, she'd immediately headed to the office to check on things as she waited for Oliver to return from camp. He'd refrained from suggesting that she might want to get some rest.

Today he busied himself fixing things around the house for Gram. And tried not to think about the way the conversation with Maggie had felt so easy. And how she'd been a force of nature handling the Pelletier wedding.

She was amazing.

But he needed to remember she'd made her choice. He'd tortured himself long enough comparing himself to Paul, imagining all the reasons she chose him. And they'd created a family, Maggie and Paul and Oliver.

What if he'd stayed in Sweet Springs?

*No, don't go there.*

He headed downstairs and smiled as he passed the framed photograph he'd purchased of Maggie in the flower field. Maggie was truly captured in her element.

The sound of the front door opening caught his attention. He looked out the living room window. Zoe was dressed in boots and jeans. Definitely not heading to the office. She must be going to ride her paint horse, Lucky Lady, who she'd rescued from the circus.

Since he'd gotten here, he'd slept late and hadn't seen her ride yet. Definitely something he'd looked forward to doing. He still had time before meeting Maggie for the deluxe tour.

Gram's door was shut. She was still sleeping and so was Hero by the sounds of his snoring. That dog had sure taken a shine to everyone here, especially Oliver, and he knew the feeling was mutual.

Walking out to the barn, he was in awe of the stunning brilliance of the flower fields. The kaleidoscope of colors bathed in the light of sunrise took his breath away.

Looking over toward Maggie's place, he saw a light on upstairs and wondered who was up this early.

The house that Maggie and her son now lived in had been a dingy one-story years ago. They must have renovated the building and added a second story. The black-and-gray exterior had just enough wood in the door and trim to give it warmth. He wondered what it looked like inside.

Nearing the corral, Zoe was just taking Lucky Lady out of the back of the barn, where the stalls were located. Her horse was the only animal left. The structure had held quite a variety of farmyard animals.

Inside, the front of the barn had been renovated and opened up. He'd learned that when he went looking for tools the other day. Fresh concrete floors had been poured. New shelves lined the walls. It could easily be sectioned off for multiple uses.

Jake stopped and leaned against a tree when he saw Zoe and Lucky Lady in the riding ring. Lucky Lady relished the carrots that Zoe was feeding her.

When it was time to ride, she fastened on her helmet. The joy on his sister's face was hard to miss.

Zoe and Lucky Lady moved in sync around the ring. Zoe

stood atop the saddle one moment. Then she was sitting back on the saddle the next. She moved with ease as she leaned off the right side of Lucky Lady and touched the ground with her hands.

Jake was impressed. Zoe rivaled anything he'd witnessed in the rodeos out West. He knew the Flint Hills Rodeo was coming up in Kansas and wished she could see it. His good friend Pastor Joe was a rodeo aficionado. Jake had often accompanied him, sometimes with a small bus of parishioners.

Zoe stood up in the saddle again, arms out, her face radiant. She looked like she was flying.

And then a realization hit him. Hard. Maybe this was what she should be doing. What she'd always wanted to do since she saw her first horse when she was six years old.

What she probably would be doing if she hadn't had to stay here in Maine to help Gram with the farm. Because Paul had moved to North Carolina for his job. And he, himself, had abandoned them.

Zoe. The cosmetology license, the accounting degree and working at the farm office. They were all distractions filling a void.

He couldn't watch her anymore. He turned and headed back to the house before she saw him. She needed her privacy. It was the least he could do for her.

There would be time when they could talk. He'd make sure of it.

Jake was sitting at the far end of the porch with a cup of coffee and a newspaper he hadn't opened when Zoe came back from riding Lucky Lady.

"Nice duds, Sis," he said.

Her cheeks flushed.

"Got time to sit for a bit?" he asked.

"Sure, let me grab some coffee. I have a minute before I have to change for the office." She slipped off her jacket and slung it over the back of the rocking chair.

Jake had been thinking about their father after their mother's death. Those last days before he left. The fight that Paul tried to stop between Jake and their father. An endless labyrinth of memories that still caused grief.

He thought about how Zoe had been the apple of his father's eye. He doted on her, and it had surprised Jake that their dad could leave her and not look back.

Zoe opened the screen door, and Hero accompanied her outside. Jake heard Gram puttering around in the kitchen, so he knew they were both up now.

He leaned down and rubbed Hero's ears. Then Jake gave him a good back scratch before slipping him one of the crunchy dog biscuits he always carried in his pocket.

"That dog is spoiled rotten," Zoe declared. "So what's up?" she asked.

"You really want to know?" Jake inhaled deeply.

"Sure." Zoe settled into the rocker and put her feet up on the railing.

"I've been thinking about Dad," said Jake simply.

"Jake!" Zoe spoke with more than a hint of disdain in her voice as she looked directly at him. "What do you wanna go and do that for?" She took a long sip of coffee.

"Okay, your feelings are crystal clear on the subject. He's persona non grata."

"Bingo!" she said. "There are a lot better things to think about." She waved away a bee that buzzed near her face.

Jake thought he caught sight of a deep fleeting sorrow in her eyes.

"I miss Mom, but I don't miss him. I have a photo of her in the office and in my bedroom," said Zoe wistfully.

He braced himself before continuing, "I miss Mom too. I tried to find him, you know."

"So did I. Then I stopped looking." Zoe stared straight ahead, no longer making eye contact with Jake.

Jake leaned forward and rubbed his hands on his jeans. "I tried to find him *not* because I wanted him to come home. But because I was so angry with him."

"You had every right to feel that way, Jake. We all did. You were the one that kept us clothed and fed until we couldn't keep it hidden anymore from school and the neighbors that he'd left." Zoe paused for a moment before continuing. "It was you who had the idea we should get ourselves out here to Gram's. Which was the best thing for us. Then Gram went and got all our stuff from the house. Our lives were such a mess back then."

Jake combed his fingers through his hair. "Dad was decent when Mom was alive."

"He was and then Mom died and he wasn't. It's like he left too, way before he physically left," Zoe said.

"And before he physically left," Jake said, "he sure went berserk, didn't he?"

"Yes, he did. One heartbreaking moment after another back then," said Zoe as she rocked in the chair.

Jake was silent. His chest tightened. He knew that his leaving had been one of her heartbreaking moments.

"I'm sorry for leaving, Zoe," Jake said so softly he doubted she would hear him.

"I know," she replied and looked at him with glistening eyes that matched his own.

Hero got up and bumped both of their legs one after the other looking for attention.

They both laughed as they patted him and told him he was a good boy.

It eased some of the tightness in his chest. And again for the millionth time, he was grateful Hero was part of his life.

Jake's coffee cup was empty, but he wasn't in any hurry to leave. "I'll be seeing you later in the office today," he told Zoe.

"Oh, that's right," Zoe said. "The deluxe tour. Barring any more emergencies, that is."

Jake saw something cross her face and wondered if Zoe was still thinking of their conversation or something else.

"Maggie is a good person, Jake. Full of compassion and a deep protective mama-bear energy. You should remember that." Zoe got up to go inside and put her hand out. "Give me your cup, and I'll put it in the sink."

"Thanks." Jake wondered why she said that about Mags. He already knew Maggie was a good person.

"I'll see you over there. Oh and it's the day Gloria brings doughnuts for everyone." She laughed. "Just sayin' I know I'll see you sooner rather than later now. Oh and Maggie's schedule is open, so you'll have a good chance to see the rest of the farm."

Jake nodded. "Appreciate the heads-up on the doughnuts." He gave her a two-finger salute as she headed inside.

He thought about his sister looking for their father. Her intense feelings about him now were not surprising. He wanted to unpack more about the past.

There'd be time for all that later on.

Maggie started getting ready for the day. Oliver would be leaving for camp soon. Then she'd meet Jake at the office. She thought about those glimpses she had caught of the old Jake yesterday. He was much more serious now. And it still seemed odd to her that he was churchy.

She twirled a pen between her fingers. Mornings, she often just sat quietly, sometimes she jotted down what was on her mind. Just free-flowing thoughts. Today though, her thoughts were more focused.

Someone else besides Jake was on her mind this morning. Before bed last night, Maggie heard Oliver double-check all the doors then go into the kitchen to check the stove. She knew what followed was seeing what was or wasn't plugged in. It was a nightly ritual he had given up for a while, but he was back at it again. It made him feel safer.

She wondered if he was having nightmares again. Maggie's own nightmares were less frequent. And fortunately, there hadn't been any triggers during the day for a while. Of course, Maggie stayed mainly on the farm. And her stress before now had been mostly about the business, nothing she felt she couldn't handle.

Maggie felt a wheelbarrow full of stress lately though. Now that Jake was back in Sweet Springs, she knew what she had to do. She had planned to tell him the truth before the wedding emergency. Today, she'd attempt to show him around again. And tell him the truth about their son.

She didn't know if Jake would be interested, but she planned to show him the piece of land where she was growing her personal flower garden. It was something outside of the business, something not profit driven. Flowers she grew just for the love of it. Flowers to give to others when the time was right. Gram had told her, "God will direct you, honey, to see who needs them."

She'd gradually begun reestablishing her connection with Him. Some days it was harder than others, given all she'd been through, to trust, but she knew deep down that was on her, not Him.

Maggie smiled. Often she felt Gram had more than enough faith for both of them.

She stood and tried to muster the strength and the courage she needed. It was past time to tell Jake her long-held secret.

Maggie walked to the office to meet Jake. It still surprised her to see him back here at Gram's.

Last month was June, the hand-holding month between spring and summer. She always felt romance was in the air, and it seemed like it was continuing this month on the farm. Couples, roaming around, leaned in close as they pointed out flowers. Some held hands, some wrapped arms around each other's waists. She felt that flowers often brought people together, even with July's rising heat and humidity and the arrival of mosquitoes in Maine.

Then she saw Jake before he saw her. Jake was wearing that Stetson again as he leaned against the office building. One knee bent with the sole of his scuffed boot on the wall. He was still so handsome.

She quickly reminded herself they had lived very different lives for the past eleven years. And he would be leaving soon. She didn't have the luxury of time to unravel the enigma of Jake Madison.

Approaching, she knew the moment he saw her, his boyish smile lighting up his face. How many women had succumbed to that smile over the years? She couldn't help but smile back.

"Zoe said there are doughnuts inside," Jake said, jerking his thumb toward the office.

"And you're out here? My, what willpower you have this morning!" Maggie recalled that he had a penchant for doughnuts and bear claws and apple fritters and every other morning pastry available on the planet.

"Thought I'd wait for you," he said as he held the door open for her.

Inside, Zoe waved her over as she held the phone out. "Distributor," Zoe mouthed quietly.

"Duty calls," she told Jake. "Be right back. Don't wait on me for the doughnuts."

"I can't resist when they're right in front of me," he said as he gave the wide-open white pastry box his full attention.

A few minutes later, Maggie returned and was informed by Zoe that Jake had cleaned off the powdered sugar from his face and hands.

"Guilty as charged," Jake admitted, somewhat sheepishly. "I await the tour, milady," he said. "Too bad, there isn't a carriage."

"Ohh," Maggie and Zoe both said in unison. They theatrically swooned as they pressed their hands over their hearts.

"What did I say?" Jake asked.

Maggie laughed. She actually thought he was blushing. "Jake, I never took you for the romantic type. But now that you mention a carriage…it's something I've wanted…"

"Me too. Ever since you mentioned it," Zoe interrupted.

"For the weddings," Maggie said. "A horse-drawn carriage all decked out in flowers to bring the bride to the ceremony."

"Like a covered wagon type of vehicle?" Jake clearly looked puzzled.

"No. Not like the Wild West. More like a Cinderella carriage to the ball," said Zoe.

Jake nodded. Maggie wondered if he got it. "It's always been the dream to have one to be a part of the wedding venue."

"Have you checked into it?" Jake asked.

"Carriages are way too pricey," Zoe said, "but we haven't given up hope."

"So, are you ready for the grand tour without the carriage ride?" Maggie asked as she grabbed her wide-brimmed straw hat from behind the counter.

"Yes, ma'am!" he said as he set his hat on his head. Again, he held the door open. Impressed, Maggie looked back at Zoe's wide-eyed expression.

As they walked, it seemed to Maggie like she was doing a lot of talking. But there was so much to show him, like the hoop houses to extend the flowers through the seasons. The propagation greenhouse.

As they walked, Maggie realized she'd have to promote someone to be the field manager when she started up the wedding venue business. Another thing on her to-do list.

Jake paused when they came to the first row of flowers. He looked back toward the driveway. "Maggie, can I suggest something?" he asked.

Surprised, she said, "Sure." She took the break to push back her hat and wipe her brow.

Jake gestured toward the entrance. "It's a long way from here to the road. I know you have a small sign, but what about adding something else?" He seemed to hesitate, as if making sure he wasn't overstepping.

"Go on," Maggie encouraged.

"I was thinking, it might be nice to have a stand out there by the main road with flowers to buy. Also, maybe a bigger sign to draw attention to the farm."

Maggie thought for a moment. "A flower stand. There could be leftover cut flowers for premade or DIY bouquets. Maybe a blackboard with what flowers are in season. Even sharing flowers with Gram and taking some home, there is always extra from the day's business."

"I'm envisioning a rustic wooden structure with possibly a couple shelves and tables," Jake continued.

Maggie sighed. "That's all well and good. I love the idea, but I have no idea how much that would cost. It isn't like I can go to a big-box hardware store and have it delivered."

"Mags, I'd build it. You could design exactly what you want, and I'd make it for you," Jake suggested.

Maggie's thoughts were spinning. This was another way to draw in more customers and have added revenue.

"I'm good with flowers but not a hammer and nails unless absolutely necessary," Maggie confessed.

"No problem. I'm great with a hammer and nails. We're bestest buddies."

"I think it's a great idea, but do you even have the time?" she asked. The other question she really wanted to ask him was just how long he was staying that he thought he could do this.

"I have nothing but time right now. My car is still in the shop. I'm working on things for Gram, but there's no reason I can't add this project. I'd really like to do this for you, Maggie. And I think it would benefit your business."

Almost speechless, she nodded. "Yes, it definitely would. But only if you have time. Wow, really, thank you for thinking of it."

"My pleasure," he beamed.

She saw Jake eye the sky and frown. "Those cumulus clouds are darkening quickly," he said. "I suggest we get inside. We're about to get soaked."

Maggie was always so aware of the weather. How had she not noticed? She glanced skyward and agreed with Jake.

The barn was closer than the house or the office. So they made a mad dash just as the first raindrops fell.

Inside the barn, Jake said he wanted to check out the tools and equipment to see what they had on hand for the project. As he headed to the shop side, Maggie called Gram to ask if Oliver could stay there when he returned from camp. She explained she and Jake were down at the barn. She was grateful that Gram hadn't taken a trip into town.

Gram told her she'd call and ask the driver to bring Oliver up to the main house.

Maggie knew *this* was the time to tell Jake. *Here. Now.*

Hero's sudden bark made her jump. He was outside, wanting to be let in. She opened the door. "How'd you know we were here, boy?" Maggie received a big slurp on her hand as a reply. Then Hero headed over toward Jake, who was sorting tools on a long plywood table.

The weight of the secret was crushing her. Her mouth felt like sandpaper. "I have something I want to talk to you about."

"Sure, be right there," Jake said.

She was starting to sweat. She was cold. No, she was hot. And her left eye started twitching.

Jake stood facing her, clearly taken aback by her sudden change in demeanor

Maggie knew their lives were about to change forever.

She prayed, no, silently pleaded, *Please help me with this. And please, Lord, make Jake understand that he can't tell Oliver. Not yet.*

She had to do it. Tell him. *Now.*

"Jake, I have something important to tell you. It's about Oliver," she said.

# *Chapter Six*

Jake focused on Maggie. She swayed. Was she dizzy? Was she going to pass out? He put his hand on her arm to steady her then led her to a bench so she could sit down before she fell down.

"What I have to say isn't easy…for me to say or you to hear," Maggie said as she wiped away tears.

Jake took a step back. "Just say it, Mags. Whatever it is."

"Jake… Oliver is your son. Paul and I always planned to tell you one day." Maggie looked down at her hands folded tightly in her lap.

"My son?" He felt all the blood drain from his face as he stepped away from her. "Really? You were going to tell me? When?" he asked.

Suddenly feeling overwhelmed, he sat down on the bench beside her.

Maggie looked at him.

"You thought you'd tell me when I got my act together, right? When I wasn't traveling on the road with the band," Jake said. "Or when you both thought I could handle it. When I wouldn't bolt as far away as possible. Because that's what I do."

"Part of that is true, Jake," Maggie said. "We were waiting for when you got your act together and came off the road. At least long enough for a decent visit."

Hero came over and laid his head on the bench between them.

They both reached out to pet him. Their fingers touched, and he gave her hand a little squeeze before pulling away.

A fleeting smile crossed her face.

"Tell me, Mags. Say the words again. I need to hear them." Jake stared intently at her.

"Oliver is your son."

Tears ran down his face, and he made no effort to wipe them away.

"Why didn't you tell me back then?" he asked quietly.

"I didn't know until after you'd left. You'd been gone for a few weeks when I found out."

"But your foster parents? What did they say?" Jake had never particularly liked them. But they provided for her.

Maggie straightened her spine. "They were mortified. A pregnant foster daughter," she said. "You know, what *would* people think?"

Jake cringed. She sounded defensive; it still hurt.

Maggie continued, "They made plans to sell their home immediately and move to Florida." Maggie's chin trembled. "They said I was eighteen, aged out of foster care so—"

"Aged out," repeated Jake. "I don't want to hear anything more about them. So, you had no one?"

He stood up, stomped across the barn to the other side and back, Hero at his heels. He sat down beside her again.

"I had Paul," she stated clearly.

Jake was full of questions that he couldn't quite formulate. They were all floating about in his mind.

"Paul found me sitting in the park one day and came over to ask how I was doing since you'd left. I told him I was staying at a friend's house. He was puzzled about that and asked me why. I burst into tears."

He popped up and paced again before returning to the bench. He nodded at Maggie to continue.

"I—I was a mess, as you can imagine."

Oh, how he wished he couldn't imagine it.

He wished he had called her after he left Sweet Springs.

"Go on, if you can," he said.

"Paul was as devastated as I was with the situation. Neither of us knew how to reach you, or where you'd gone. You'd disappeared. Right then and there, your brother offered to marry me."

Jake shook his head. He knew his brother. It was all playing out like a movie in his mind.

"I said that I couldn't possibly marry him," Maggie said. Hero laid his head on her foot.

"But Paul was persuasive. And I finally agreed. We went to Gram and said we were going to get married. She didn't ask questions. Maybe she assumed we were part of the reason you had left."

"Does Gram know about Oliver being my son?"

"No. We never told her. I don't know if she ever guessed it. She never asked. I just hope… I just hope she forgives me." Tears slid down her cheeks.

"What about Zoe? Does she know?" he asked next.

Maggie visibly tensed. "Yes, she was my only confidante. *Our* only confidante. Please don't be angry with her," she implored.

He'd deal with his sister later. He simply said, "I'm glad you had someone. You *both* had someone."

Maggie's shoulders visibly relaxed.

"So you married my brother," he said.

Jake remembered how devastated he'd been when the news reached him. He wasn't proud of his behavior afterward. He didn't call to congratulate them. He'd lived life on the wild side, drinking, doing whatever he could to stay busy. He'd wanted to avoid thinking about the marriage and how it happened so quickly. And no, his behavior wasn't anything he wanted to talk or even think about.

Maggie continued, "Paul got an office job with a large company and was transferred to North Carolina before Oliver was born. Gram was pretty unhappy about it, but the pay was substantial, and we had a baby coming."

"Wait," Jake stopped her. "Paul went to the university, didn't he? He wanted to be an English professor. He was always fascinated by medieval literature."

Jake remembered how he teased Paul about being able to quote lines from Chaucer.

"No, Paul didn't go to the university to become a professor. He needed a more practical way to make a living." Maggie looked away. "Eventually he got a degree at a technical college."

"So, you didn't have any more children?" Jake asked her.

"Paul couldn't have children," replied Maggie in a neutral tone.

"So, my brother married you knowing I had gotten you pregnant. Raised my son."

"Paul was a good father and husband," Maggie told him with conviction.

Jake stood up, his eyes closed. He stayed that way for a brief moment then looked at her.

"Mags, I'm so sorry." His apology was a decade late. It must sound like just words. Hollow words.

She nodded.

So much pain swirled around them it was palpable.

Jake grasped the gravity of his past actions. It was beginning to sink in deeply how much his behavior affected the lives of those he most cared for.

"I'm sorry too, Jake," she said, barely audible.

"Let me be clear, Maggie. You have nothing to be sorry about." He truly meant that.

"Regardless, Jake, I do have something to ask you. And I really need you to understand."

Jake sat down. "What is it?" he asked, looking into her blue eyes, which were filling up with unshed tears.

"We can't tell Oliver about you being his father right now. Not yet. I'm trying to avoid exposing him to any dramatic changes or stress in his life right now. He's still recovering from the fire and the car accident. I hope you'll understand. Please, Jake," Maggie pleaded.

Maggie looked terror-stricken, as if he wouldn't understand, or worse, he'd deny her request. That shattered him into a million pieces.

"Of course," he answered quickly, "I understand. His recovery is important. I want to understand more about what he's been through. I may not have the right to ask. So it's only if you feel you want to share it with me."

The moments of silence while waiting for her answer were painful.

"Yes, of course, Jake, you're his father. What exactly do you want to know?" Maggie trembled.

"How is Oliver doing? Really?"

Maggie needed to tell him the whole truth. "After the fire, he really struggled. He'd get up in the middle of the night to go to the bathroom and wave his hands in the air to see if he felt heat. He'd sniff the air to see if he smelled smoke. I often overheard his loud repetition of the day's events every night before he went to sleep. He tried to force himself to remember everything he could. He was terrified of waking up with more of his memory gone."

"And now?" Jake's heart pounded in his chest.

"Now, it seems he's regressed a bit recently. He's checking the cords on the appliances to make sure they're plugged in properly. He's afraid they might catch fire. He's double-checking the locks on the doors. He may be having nightmares again. I noticed that he's been more withdrawn at times." Maggie stopped there.

"This is a lot to process," said Jake. "And you don't know why he had the reaction that he had to me the other day?"

Maggie shook her head as she patted Hero.

"Do you have any other questions right now?" Maggie asked.

"Yes. Does Oliver remember Paul?" Jake wanted to know. "I know he has spotty amnesia."

One more devastating thing that gutted him.

"He has partial amnesia from a beam hitting his head when we were trying to escape the fire in North Carolina. Also from being in the car with Paul the night of the crash that took Paul's life. He doesn't remember things due to the trauma of both of those events in his life. No, he doesn't have memories of Paul. I don't know if he'll ever get them back." Maggie started to tremble again. "It's all too much for a little boy to endure," she said fighting back tears.

Taking her hand in his, he asked, "Maggie, can you ever forgive me?"

"Jake, I already have," she said softly.

"I don't deserve it, but I'll take that for now," he said. He let go of her hand and stood up. "Maggie, I'm a different person now than the one who left a year after high school. All I can say is that I'll try my best to show you the man I am now by my actions, not just my words."

"I've changed as well, Jake. We're both different people than we used to be," she said.

Sadness tinged her voice.

Jake looked into her eyes. "Maggie, thank you for telling me. I do understand." He just wanted to be a part of Oliver's life. And Maggie's life as well, whatever that looked like. Right now he had no idea.

She looked exhausted.

"Are you okay?" Jake asked.

"As good as I can be. You?" Maggie asked in return.

Jake noted the skin under her eyes looked dark and bruised. "Same. I think I need to go see Zoe right now, if that's all right with you?" he asked.

Maggie nodded. "Jake. Be good to her. She wanted to tell you. We all did. She loves you." Maggie looked like she wanted to say more but stopped herself.

He nodded. "I know."

Jake heard Maggie sigh as he bent over to gently kiss the top of her head. He wished he could find Oliver and do the same even though they didn't yet know each other well.

Maggie rose slowly. "I'll head home soon." She reached down to pat Hero, and he nudged her hand with his nose.

"We'll talk again soon, all right, Mags?"

"Yes, that sounds good," Maggie replied.

"Until tomorrow then." He realized his voice sounded as broken and drained as he felt.

Without putting on his jacket or hat, he whistled for Hero, and they headed out of the barn into the rain.

Maggie stayed in the barn a little longer after Jake left with Hero. She felt both exhausted and relieved at the same time. A whopper of a stress headache was beginning. The rain pounding on the metal roof of the barn wasn't helping. Every muscle ached. She needed to go home, take some acetaminophen and close her eyes. No going back to work for her today. Thankfully, Oliver would be staying with Gram for a little while.

First, though, she needed to get a hold of Zoe. Pronto. It couldn't wait till she made it home.

Maggie texted her.

He knows. On his way there now.

He knows?!! How did he take it? Angry with us? You OK?

I'm OK. Said he was glad you were there for us. But he's overloaded. Needs you though. Be patient.

I see him. More later.

Maggie stood up slowly and saw a yellow slicker hanging on a hook. She made her way over to it, thankful it was there.

Two hours later, asleep on the couch, Maggie bolted upright when she heard the ping of her cell phone.

Jake wants to tell Gram—alone—tonight. Can I bring Oliver home & we can talk later? Oh, and Hero too?

Maggie responded, Okay.

What choice did she have? She and Zoe had wanted to be there when Gram found out. Zoe must not have been able to talk him out of it.

She grabbed a sweater and her cell phone and headed out to the porch. Everything was so lush and green after the rain. A beautiful Maine evening. It was six o'clock and so still. Another couple of hours of dusk left. Right now the horizon was a lovely muted gray and soft pink.

Maggie wondered if Oliver had eaten. Gram was all about feeding people. She felt relieved at the thought. Her own stomach wasn't up to food.

She heard Zoe and Oliver before she saw them. Zoe was talking him out of something by the sounds of it. She was wonderful with her nephew.

And she noticed the developing bond between Oliver and Hero. It was almost as if they'd grown up together.

"Mom. M-Mom. We saw earthwor-r-r-ms! I wanted to sh-sh-show you." Oliver blinked hard as he tried to speak. His thoughts were getting ahead of his words. "Aunt Z-Z-Zoe said we didn't have a prop-prop-er home for them."

*Thank you, Aunt Zoe, for that,* thought Maggie.

Oliver was not being derailed though. "Let's make one, okay?"

*Do they have earthworm homes? Like ant farms?*

"How about we start with another kind of pet?" Maggie suggested.

"Like Hero?" Oliver's eyes grew wide.

"Not a dog. Or an earthworm. More like a turtle or a hamster or a fish," Maggie said. She looked at Zoe, who was clearly trying not to laugh.

"Fish! Wa-water is good. Stops fires. And I'll f-f-feed it tomorrow and—"

"Whoa, young man! Slow down. I think we ought to wait a bit. Okay?"

Oliver was clearly disappointed. "Okay. I have H-Hero as a fr-friend. C-c-can I go play video games now? I ate already."

"Sure, but first, what does Zoe have in the bag there?" Maggie inquired.

"Anyone up for a milkshake?" She pulled out containers of mocha and vanilla ice cream. "I thought you might want this, Maggie."

"Yes, Mom," Maggie teased. "Seriously, I can't think of anything better. What do you say, Oliver? You shouldn't have one so close to bedtime, but we can make an exception just for tonight."

Oliver nodded his head vigorously then said, "C-C'mon, Aunt Zoe," as he pulled on her shirtsleeve to guide her inside the house.

"Be back soon," Zoe said as she held the door open for Hero to follow them inside.

Maggie welcomed another few moments of peace.

"Here we come," announced Zoe as Oliver held open the door and kept two hands on his much smaller milkshake.

"C-c-can I—I take mine upstairs with H-Hero?" Oliver asked.

As much as she wanted to hear what Zoe had to say, she also didn't want a milkshake spilled on the keyboard.

"How about staying out here till you finish?" Maggie suggested.

Oliver was clearly disappointed again. First, he had to wait on the pet and now he had to wait on his computer games. Oliver plunked down on the top porch step and took his first slurp. Hero lay down beside him with his paws hanging over the steps.

"Oliver, I use apps to learn tricks for riding Lucky Lady," Zoe said.

Oliver shook his head. "Lucky Lady is big and sc-sc-scary!" he declared.

"I think you two might like each other once you get to know each other in the future," Zoe said as she took a sip of her milkshake.

Maggie couldn't get Oliver anywhere near Lucky Lady. Part of her was okay with that. One less worry. Still, it would be good to someday get him over his fear of horses, if possible.

"Oliver, what's your favorite computer game?" Zoe asked.

"Dragons. Fire-breathing dragons!" Oliver shouted. "I hunt them and stop them. Can I go play now?"

"Yes, honey. Have fun," Maggie told him.

She waited until she heard him rinse his glass at the kitchen sink and head upstairs before she turned to Zoe. "Are you thinking what I'm thinking?"

Zoe nodded. "Stopping dragons, stopping fire."

"And earlier," Maggie added, "he wanted a fish because 'water is good. Stops fires.'"

Zoe nodded. "Earlier, I didn't want him to pick up on my stress at Gram's. But now that Jake knows, there should be less stress, right?"

"What if Jake changes his mind about telling Oliver?" Maggie fidgeted with the hem of her sweater.

"We both know that Jake wouldn't do anything to hurt you or Oliver."

Maggie nodded. "I know," she said, not reminding Zoe that Jake'd broken her heart years ago. "How did it go this afternoon? Dare I ask?"

"It was hard. He asked a lot of questions." Zoe hesitated.

"Like what?" Maggie prompted.

"About my knowing the truth all along. If you and Paul were happy. I said I thought so. Toward the end of the conversation, he was clearly exhausted. He asked me why I didn't tell him the truth." Zoe finished her shake and set it down.

"Hmm," said Maggie.

"I said we couldn't find him to tell him. That he went away for a long time. He said that we'd all decided for him."

Maggie interrupted. "We did decide for him."

"No, it was decided for Oliver. When Jake resurfaced at Paul's funeral, he was still in no way ready to learn he had a son. Seemed like he was still chasing fame down the road. And he needed to heal from our father singling him out so often when he was angry." Zoe paused. "Then he thanked me for being there for you and Paul. He gave me the biggest, longest hug in the history of hugs."

Maggie's heart ached for all of them.

Maggie and Zoe sat quietly together. The only sounds to be heard were crickets, whip-poor-wills, and owls singing their nighttime songs.

"Do you want me to go with you when you face Gram tonight? Or would you rather stay here?" Maggie asked.

"That's super kind of you to offer. But you've been through it all and back again today," Zoe said.

Maggie nodded.

Zoe continued, "And tomorrow is the Sweet Springs Summer Celebration and if I have any say, I'm getting my brother to go with us to the fireworks "

"There will be a lot of people. Jake knows Oliver is his son but he can't say anything, yet. That won't be easy for him," Maggie said.

*No*, she thought, *it won't be easy for any of us.*

# *Chapter Seven*

Jake had tossed and turned all night. He'd dreamed that he and his brother were kids again. They jumped off the old tire swing. Drove the four-wheeler down the old logging roads. Fished in the river. Then he dreamed of Paul and Oliver doing all of the same things.

Jake missed his brother every day. It was even worse here in Maine, where memories were everywhere he looked.

He had already missed so much of Oliver's life that Paul had experienced. Jake prayed for the chance to connect with Oliver.

Jake also dreamed of Maggie last night. Memories flowed of eating ice cream together while sitting on the bridge over the river. Holding hands while walking around town.

He studied himself in the mirror. He looked the same, but he didn't feel the same. It was one thing to think something might be true. It was another to have it confirmed.

He had a son.

Soon the Sweet Springs Summer Celebration would begin. He wanted to share it all with Oliver and his family.

Glancing at the time, he knew Zoe was already at work.

Gram greeted him in the kitchen. "Good morning! How are you?" She studied him as closely as he'd studied himself in the mirror earlier.

"I'm all right, I think," he said honestly. "Do you, by chance, need the truck today?"

"I have no plans today. Keys are in the bowl," she said.

"Thanks, Gram. Just thought I'd get some air and check on the progress of my car. See what's changed in town."

"That's fine." Gram sounded like she was measuring her words before she continued.

He waited.

"Zoe wanted me to tell you that Pastor Joe called. He couldn't reach you on your cell. So he called on the landline. He said he was calling because he wondered what you planned to do about the job offers in Kansas?"

Jake chewed his bottom lip.

Gram continued, "He said some of them begin next month in and around Manhattan, Kansas, and some in September. He thought you probably planned to be back by now when you applied. And you should call them pronto to set up interviews." She wiped her hands on a gingham dish towel.

"I see," said Jake. He wasn't sure how he felt about the news.

Gram put her hand on his arm. "Jake, honey, let's sit a spell. I want to know how you *really* are this morning." She took off her apron and set two cups on the table.

"My best answer is, I don't know," Jake said as he ran his fingers through his hair and sat down.

"Fair enough. You've had a lot to deal with since you've been back in Sweet Springs," she said. "Can't be easy."

"I had a lot of work to do on myself, I was such a mess emotionally when I left," he said. "And now that I'm back, I have more to work on. I'm trying to be a better person than who I was. I want to make amends. Work on forgiveness." He attempted a smile.

"And did you work on it? And are you willing to keep working on it now?" Gram asked as she poured the tea.

"Yes. I'm a work in progress, that's for sure," Jake said as he warmed his hands on the cup.

"Aren't we all?" Gram said. "He knows that, you know. Have

you spoken to Him about this? About what you're feeling? God is a good listener."

Jake was silent for a moment before answering. "Yes. I think I need to go to His house today to have a good, long chat."

Gram nodded. "Sounds good. He might have some ideas for you. I think you're going to be all right," Gram said with conviction. "I'm here. Your family is here. I think you're where you should be right now."

Jake sent up a silent prayer of thanks. He asked to be worthy of this mercy and grace he felt continually from his family.

Before he left the house, Gram gave him a big hug that warmed him body, mind and soul. It was exactly what he needed.

In town, he thought he'd go check on his car. But Matt's garage was closed. The sign said he was gone up north for a week to ten days for a family wedding. Jake checked his messages, and sure enough, Matt had emailed him, telling him he'd be in touch when he got back in town.

Jake parked Gram's truck near the hardware store. The town was decked out with flags, and there were booths set up around the town square for food and crafts.

He felt the urge to wander around. Not a lot had changed. There were a few different businesses that he could see. But mostly things were the same.

What if he had never left or he'd come back before Maggie and Paul were married…

*Enough.*

Jake headed to Old Grace Church. A place where God had been listening to folks for a good many years.

He missed Hero but leaving him with Gram today was a good idea. The news of him being Oliver's father was a lot for her to digest as well. Hero could be good company.

Zoe would also probably turn up to see her at lunch time, if he knew his sister.

He walked inside the sanctuary. The worn wood of the pews matched the ceiling beams and posts that were carved with lilies. A choir box graced the second floor. Jake was drawn to the front. The altar was bathed in the warm rich colors from the stained-glass windows.

Hat in his hand, he suddenly wished he had his guitar. He yearned to play a song. To write a song. It had been a while.

Then he spied the piano. Looking around, he called out, "Hello?" but no one replied.

Jake sat on the piano bench and began to play. And sing. Hymns followed by songs he'd written. Music poured out of him and filled the room.

When he finished, tears rolling down his face, he heard someone gently clapping.

Embarrassed, he wiped his wet cheeks. He saw a man sitting in the front row, dressed casually in navy pants and a white button-down shirt,

"No need to feel shy," the man said. "You played to the Lord, and I know He was as impressed as I was."

The man approached him and held out his hand. "I'm Pastor Luke."

"Jake." He shook Pastor Luke's hand. "Thank you for the church being open today."

The pastor pushed his glasses up on his nose. "I know lots of folks say it isn't safe these days to keep the church open. But it's important to me. Doesn't mean I don't worry. I'd sure hate to have anything happen to this beautiful church."

Jake nodded as he sat down beside the pastor. They both looked toward the altar.

"If music isn't a part of your life, it should be," Pastor Luke said softly.

Jake rubbed his temple. "We've had quite a relationship, music and I. Down a rocky path, then I made my way back where I felt more comfortable with its presence in my life. And now, I'd say, music and I are good friends. We weathered many a storm though. I've just returned from working with a music ministry in Guatemala City."

"You don't say, Jake. And do you call this part of Maine home?"

*Home?* Jake wasn't sure if he even had a home anymore.

"I'm visiting from Kansas, but I grew up here in Sweet Springs. I'm visiting family in town. Then I'll be heading back West." Jake realized he had no idea when. It would have to be soon to secure a job. Set up interviews. Yes, right, that was what he'd planned.

"Not many Maine folks wear Stetsons around here. You have family in town, you said?" Pastor Luke asked.

Jake nodded. "You know my grandmother, Yvonne Madison."

"Ah, yes, she's a wonderful person. Everyone I know has the highest regard for her." Pastor Luke paused. "Yesterday I learned that our little church needs a new choir director."

Surprised, Jake just nodded.

"It's a temporary position," said Pastor Luke. "For July and August. Miss Mary Ouellette has decided to retire and is heading out on a seniors' cruise. I'll look to be hiring someone in the fall when I can give it my full attention."

"Well, as I said, I'm heading back to Kansas soon," said Jake.

"You probably have a job out there in Kansas, no doubt," the Pastor said.

"Not exactly," Jake admitted.

"I see." Pastor Luke looked thoughtful.

Jake knew he was staring at the pastor like he had two heads, but he couldn't help it.

Pastor Luke laughed. Then he stood up and put his hand on Jake's shoulder. "Mull it over this weekend. Please know, you're welcome to come back and play the piano anytime. Feel free to contact me with any questions about the temporary position."

Jake thought he heard the good pastor chuckle softly as he left. Jake sat in the pew a little while longer, hat in his hand, before heading back to the farm.

The day of the Sweet Springs Summer Celebration, Maggie woke up feeling restless.

She'd tried hard not to make Oliver feel uncomfortable last night and this morning as she dealt with all her emotions from telling Jake the truth yesterday. Part of her had just wanted to hug her son and tell him how much she loved him over and over again. Another part just wanted to collapse in a puddle of tears on the kitchen floor. She did neither.

Gram had been on her mind from the moment she woke up. She'd prayed that all had gone as well as it possibly could with her and Jake and Zoe at the house last night.

Oliver was running around with Hero in the yard. She was happy to see him spending more time outside in the fresh air. They both came running when she stepped off the front porch.

"Fancy a walk before we head to town for the festivities?" she asked. Her son nodded and motioned for Hero to follow them.

Maggie knew it would be more of a walk by herself as the two of them ran all over the place. Walking past the flower fields, the office and nearing Gram's house, she hesitated. She wondered how Gram felt about the whole situation. It made her nervous.

"There's GG!" yelled Oliver as he and Hero ran straight for her.

Part of her wanted to burst into tears at the sight of Gram standing by the rose bushes holding her pruning scissors.

Oliver jumped up and down as she pulled out a cookie from one front pocket and a crunchy dog treat from the other.

Gram stepped forward and threw her arms around Maggie. Neither said a word as Gram gave Maggie a big bear hug.

"Gram—"

"Shh. I love you, and I *know* everything you did was for your boy. You're family, and nothing you could ever do would change how I feel about you. I was hoping I'd see you before we all headed to town. We'll have a chin wag about things in the future." Gram drew back then kissed her cheek.

Her kind gesture and healing words buoyed Maggie's spirits tenfold. She held back her tears and hugged Gram tightly.

Fairy lights and flags were strung throughout downtown Sweet Springs. Maggie overheard people saying that the fireworks were the biggest ever. The air was filled with anticipation as dusk drew closer.

Jake caught up with Maggie and Oliver. He and Hero had just made a stop at the hardware store. Jake had his Bullmastiff on a leash and planned to take him back home before the fireworks began. Then he'd return to join everyone.

"There's Auntie Z-Zoe, Mom," Oliver said as he patted his mother's arm. Hero barked. "D-do you see her? C-c-can I go over there? C-can I take Hero?"

"All right but I want you back with me well before the fireworks. I'll text her, and if she forgets, will you be sure and remind her?" Maggie asked. Fireworks were one thing they hadn't seen in person yet. Oliver had watched them on television, so she thought he'd enjoy them.

"Keep Hero on the leash and stay close to Aunt Zoe. I want to take Hero home before the fireworks start, okay, bud?" said Jake.

Oliver nodded vigorously. Then he was off, holding Hero's leash, before Maggie could get in a side hug.

Her stomach tightened a little as she texted Zoe. There were so many people. Oliver didn't usually have the courage to brave crowds like this without her, but with Hero at his side today, he did. She should just be thankful. And he'd be with Zoe too. She needed to stop worrying.

"Let's find the Moo Dairy food truck before I take Hero home," said Jake.

Maggie smiled. "Raspberry ice cream in a waffle cone?"

"You know me well," Jake laughed as he tried to maneuver them through the crowd to the line of food trucks.

"Some things never change," she said. And it was true even after all these years. But she couldn't help thinking that the opposite was true as well.

Maggie stopped to pick up a few business cards at some busy booths, looking for possible vendors for the wedding venue.

"Business is always on your mind," Jake teased.

Maggie made a face at him and heard him laugh.

Jake stopped at the Maple Moose booth to buy Gram some maple syrup. They made several more stops before reaching the ice cream truck. People kept stopping them to welcome Jake back as a celebrity.

Sometimes she forgot about his status as a country rock star.

Suddenly, there was a large boom of fireworks. It was just a trial run before tonight's big event, but it made Maggie uneasy.

She saw Jake rub his neck and could tell he felt the same. "I should have taken Hero home sooner," Jake said.

"Let's catch up with the others quickly," Maggie said. She'd feel better with Oliver and Hero back safely by their sides.

Maggie felt Jake's hand on her back as they wove through the crowd.

Soon Maggie spied Zoe and a couple of friends. But where was Oliver? Where was Hero?

Maggie called out "Zoe!" before she reached her.

Zoe turned around, smiling.

"Where's Oliver and Hero?" Maggie asked in a shaky voice.

Zoe looked puzzled. "I don't know. Last time I saw Oliver, he was with you. I don't know about Hero."

"Oliver saw you and headed your way with Hero. We were

all supposed to meet up before the fireworks. I texted you." Maggie could feel her blood pressure rising.

"I never saw him." Zoe checked her text messages. "I didn't hear the ping!" Zoe's voice rose.

Jake looked at Maggie and asked, "Is Oliver afraid of fireworks?"

"He enjoys them on television. He's not usually afraid of loud noises," Maggie said, feeling faint.

Jake took charge. "We need to divide and conquer. Zoe, you and your friends go that way, and Maggie and I will go this way."

Seeing the concern on all their faces as they fanned out quickly elevated Maggie's fear.

Jake and Maggie pushed their way through the crowd. Just then her phone rang. Maggie handed the phone to Jake. "I'm too nervous—you answer it."

Jake touched her arm as he read the text.

"It's Zoe. No sign of Oliver or Hero. She asked if they should alert the police," Jake told Maggie as they reached the edge of the crowd.

"You don't think he wandered near the river, do you?" Maggie asked.

"I don't know," said Jake. "I can check there."

"I'm going with you," Maggie said.

As they headed toward the edge of the riverbank, Jake stopped her. "Mags, Zoe wants to know about calling in more help. What do you think?"

Maggie stopped. It was getting dark now. She looked up at a whooshing sound in the air. An owl was on the prowl for his dinner. It was humid and sweltering. Her heart pounded as fear ricocheted inside her.

She didn't know where her son was.

She nodded vigorously. "We need all the help we can get," she told Jake.

He texted Zoe that they'd make the call.

Maggie suddenly seized Jake's arm. "Wait!" she said loudly. "I hear something."

Jake stopped and closed his eyes. "It sounds like Oliver! It's coming from that direction."

They both ran toward the riverbank. Maggie felt panicked and breathless every step of the way.

Jake yelled, "I see them!"

Maggie couldn't believe her eyes. Hero had a hold of Oliver's shirt in his mouth as he tried to drag him out of the water.

Jake reached them first and pulled Oliver up on the grass to safety.

Maggie quickly sat on the ground near him. She soon began rocking a sobbing Oliver in her lap. "It's all right, honey," she said. "It's all right now," Maggie kept repeating.

Jake hugged his dog. "Good boy, Hero! I'm so glad you're safe too!" he said. Hero rested his head on Jake's shoulder then slumped down as if totally exhausted.

"Are you hurt? " Maggie asked Oliver in an urgent tone. "Can you tell us what happened? Oh, Oliver! I was so worried."

"He-Hero s-s-saved me. I—I sl-slipped into the river. H-Hero jumped in and gr-grabbed me." Oliver opened his mouth wide and clamped it shut, biting down hard. "He wouldn't l-l-let go. For—for a m-minute, we didn't m-move. The wa-water p-pulled us."

Maggie gasped.

"I—I—I was s-s-standing on the edge of the rocks, and I—I—I—I got a cramp in my l-leg and s-slipped." Oliver started coughing.

Maggie's voice came out in a high pitch. "Standing here near the rapids? You know better than…"

She felt Jake's hand on her shoulder and looked at him. He subtly shook his head. He was right, now was not the time to chastise him.

Jake took off his shirt and handed it to Maggie.

"Let's put this on you," said Maggie as she helped Oliver put on Jake's dry shirt.

As Oliver began buttoning it up, Jake said, "I'll text Zoe we've found him."

Zoe texted back, asking if they were bringing Oliver straight home.

Maggie nodded. "Ask her to ring our neighbor, Carly. She's a physician assistant. I want her opinion on Oliver tonight."

"Will do," said Jake. "And I'll ask Zoe to bring me a dry shirt."

After the phone call, he knelt down on the grass and hugged Oliver. "How are you feeling now ?" he asked.

"I—I—I have a l-l-little cr-cramp here." Oliver pointed to his calf. "B-b-b-better now but I—I—I don't th-think I can stand up."

"That's all right, you don't have to," said Maggie. She looked at Jake. "We have to get him home."

Jake nodded. "Is it all right if I carry you to the car, Oliver?"

Oliver looked up at Jake in relief and nodded. Jake scooped him up.

Maggie noticed Hero seemed to wobble a bit when he walked. She wished she could scoop him up as well as they headed back to the car.

The fireworks were beginning, but Maggie didn't think any of them noticed.

When their neighbor, Carly Laurent, left after checking Oliver, Maggie tried to relax. Carly had advised to keep him awake a little longer, though she felt no bumps on his head from any rocks. She told Maggie to call the doctor in the morning if she had concerns and reminded her that she was just next door if they needed anything else.

Carly also advised Jake to get Hero checked by his veterinarian after she noticed some stiffness and soreness in his jaw and she'd also listened to his chest as well.

Jake had on the shirt that Zoe gave him from home.

Oliver sat quietly on the couch in his pajamas.

Everyone was gathered in the living room. Gram and Zoe were cooing over Hero being a true hero tonight. Jake's dog, however, only had eyes for Oliver and wouldn't leave his side.

Jake joined Maggie in the kitchen as she was getting refreshments.

"It was so unlike him to wander off like that," Maggie said. "I have to ask him what he was thinking."

"I'm not so sure now is a good time to do that," Jake said.

Maggie looked over to the living room. Oliver was sitting on the sofa petting Hero.

"I have to," said Maggie. "Don't you want to know why too?"

"Everyone does, I imagine," said Jake.

Maggie brought Oliver some cookies and crackers with cheese, which she set out on the coffee table.

She sat down beside Oliver, who cuddled up under her arm. "How are you feeling, honey? Is your leg cramp all gone?" she asked.

"Yes. I—I'm okay," he replied.

"Can you tell us why you went to the riverbank? That's not like you to wander off and not tell me," she said softly.

Oliver cast his eyes downward.

"S-s-s-someone said they hoped the—the—the new fireworks didn't c-c-catch fire. All—all the people. I—I couldn't f-find anyone. It was so loud and scary."

Maggie hugged him closer. "I'm so sorry that scared you so much. It wasn't like the fireworks on television, was it?" she said.

"N-no," Oliver said.

Maggie tried to reassure him. "We don't have to go to see fireworks in person."

Oliver was silent.

"Maybe he should have a phone?" Jake suggested.

"I think so too," Maggie agreed.

"Maggie, honey?" She felt Gram's hand on her shoulder. She looked up at her and tried to focus on what she was saying. "I think everyone is exhausted. We should probably go home now," said Gram.

Maggie nodded.

"We're close, sweet girl, if you need anything. And we'll see you both tomorrow," Gram said.

Maggie hugged Gram tight before she headed toward the door.

Next she hugged Zoe, who told her, "You should sleep in tomorrow morning. It's a special day after all."

Maggie blinked.

Zoe laughed. "It's your birthday."

"I completely forgot!" Maggie exclaimed.

After Gram and Zoe left, she looked at Oliver sleeping on the couch. Hero sat nearby. She decided to stay close to Oliver and sleep in the chair.

Heading out to the foyer to say good-night to Jake, she heard him call Hero more than once to get him to leave.

Maggie knelt down and looked into Hero's eyes and told him everything was all right thanks to him. Hero slurped her face, which made Maggie laugh, then he joined Jake.

"Thank you for everything, Jake, and Hero too," she added. "If you hadn't been there, if you hadn't brought Hero to Maine..." Maggie shuddered.

"None of us had any idea this would happen, Mags," Jake said as he hugged her good-night.

The truth was, she knew she had to do better to protect Oliver.

# Chapter Eight

First thing in the morning, Jake called Maggie to check on Oliver. She said he was nearly back to his normal self.

Next Jake took Hero to the vet to get him checked out. He did seem to have a sore jaw. The vet put him on a nearly liquid diet until his next checkup.

Back home, Hero wasn't having any of the pureed salmon, rice and peas with a touch of olive oil. It wasn't okay with Hero until he licked some off Jake's fingers then he ate all of it. As Jake sat on the floor coaxing Hero to eat, he sent up prayers of thanks that Oliver and Hero were all right.

Gram was a busy woman this morning. The three-tier German chocolate cake on the counter looked like something from a magazine. On the side counter sat a container of marshmallow fluff for whoopie pies, which he knew Maggie loved, and a bag of multi-colored balloons.

Even if Jake hadn't remembered that today was Maggie's birthday, he would have been reminded by the activity in the kitchen. Gram took birthdays very seriously.

Jake carried that festive feeling with him as he headed out the door. It was a welcome distraction from what happened last night.

It was a shame he wouldn't have the flower stand by the road ready in time.

Just before noon, to Jake's surprise, Oliver showed up with

Hero at his side. He wished the boy would rest today, and he planned to encourage him to do just that.

Jake noticed that Oliver was overcoming his shyness as his curiosity brought him closer to Jake…and his building tools. Jake began putting out and naming his tools, which Oliver seemed so interested in. He set them up on a plywood table sitting on two sawhorses—hammer, screwdriver, wrenches, pliers…

Oliver was a quick learner and liked finding the right tool when asked. Every time he did, Oliver's smile lit up Jake's whole world.

Zoe once described Oliver as a skittish colt. It was something Jake kept in the back of his mind. Trust and rapport took time to build, and he was more than willing to take it as slowly as needed.

After a while, Jake saw Oliver tiring. He was not surprised.

"Oliver, I think you need to get some rest."

At that, Oliver yawned. "I—I'll help p-put away the t-tools, Uncle Jake."

"I can do that. You just make sure you rest a bit, all right?" Jake asked.

Oliver nodded. "C-can we work m-more l-later?" he asked.

Jake checked the time on his cell phone. "Maybe, when I get back after three o'clock."

Oliver grinned, and he and Hero headed off toward Gram's house.

Right now, Jake had an urgent matter. He didn't have a present for Maggie's birthday.

After he cleared the worksite, he stopped to see Zoe at the office, making sure Maggie wasn't nearby to overhear their conversation.

"It's not like I can give her flowers. And by the looks of Gram's kitchen, there's no need for more chocolate." Jake scratched his head.

Zoe laughed. "You haven't bought many presents for women, have you?"

She hit the nail on the head. Gift cards, tickets to events, boxes of chocolate were common gifts for the women he'd worked with. The women he dated, presents were usually flowers or dinner. Nothing really personal because he'd never really felt deeply for anyone he'd dated, since Maggie.

"Think with your heart when you're trying to woo a woman. What does she like? What would make her happy? And why didn't you try to think of something earlier?" Zoe sighed loudly.

"I didn't say anything about wooing anyone. I'm talking about a birthday present. I thought I could get a little help from my sister." Curious, he asked, "What did you get her?"

"Oliver and I bought a vintage leather-bound book of Victorian flower lore. It has all the names and meanings of flowers. She loves to look up that information. We found one from an antiquarian book dealer in Portland. Kinda pricey but gorgeous. It was actually Oliver who thought of it. Which reminds me, I better wrap it up," she said.

The bell jangled at the office door. A young woman was attempting to navigate a stroller in front of her and a wagon of plants behind her. It looked like a disaster waiting to happen.

Jake rushed over to help the struggling mother. The woman thanked him profusely. He waited until Zoe began ringing up the mother's sale then called out, "Thanks for your help, Zoe," and stepped outside.

Outside, he walked on the gravel road toward the old wood lot beyond Gram's house. It was secluded enough to feel private, a hidden retreat. There was a stone wall which separated the field from the wood lot. He'd often daydreamed of building a house there.

As a kid, he had always loved a particular old oak tree. It was the same tree that he, Paul and Zoe had hung a tire swing on. The problem was that none of them could tie the rope tight enough. Invariably they ended up on the ground. Or rolling off somewhere with the tire.

There were memories everywhere.

Sitting on the ground in front of the tree, he thought his sister had the right idea. Flowers made Mags happy. What did she talk about on the tour? Irrigation, greenhouses, some hoop things and venues.

Wait. Her eyes had lit up when she talked about creating wedding venues. Suddenly he had an epiphany. Actually two of them. One for her birthday and one for something else that he'd need Matt's help with.

Pulling out his phone, he searched for recommended books for opening a wedding venue. She'd said she hadn't had time to research resources and what others were doing yet.

Jake called several bookstores and found one on Route One that had several books he was looking for. He could easily make it there and back before the birthday celebration at the house tonight. The clerk said she'd be happy to hold the books for him.

He called Zoe next. For once, it didn't go to voicemail. "You're a genius," he told her.

"Of course I am." She laughed.

"And so modest too. I know what to get Maggie, thanks to you."

"Oh, the wooing present?" Zoe teased.

"Hanging up now. Thank you. See you at dinner." He smiled when he heard her asking what the present was as he ended the call.

He hoped Gram's truck was free. Boy, he *really* needed his car back. Hopefully that would happen soon, and then he could talk to Matt about his idea for a project as well.

Jake ran back to the house. He didn't have any time to waste. Gram laughed when he asked about her truck. "Doesn't look like I'm going anywhere today." She wiped her hands on an apron already dusty with flour.

"No, ma'am, it sure doesn't," he said. "I'm heading out to get Maggie's birthday present."

"Men! Always last minute. Did I tell you that your grandfather bought some of my presents at the gas station? Last-minute flowers, candy or knickknacks. I still have a half dozen plastic animals with bobble heads for the dash of the pickup." She laughed softly at the memory. "The good news is that he got better with age. I don't know if the presents got better."

Jake always loved how his grandparents had teased each other endlessly. Everyone knew how much in love they were. He missed his grandfather. Even though he'd died when Jake was a boy, he had cherished every memory.

Just then, he noticed the finished whoopie pies sitting on the counter beside her.

"No, sir, those are for Maggie's party." Gram snapped the dish towel at him.

"You've always had eyes in the back of your head, Gram."

"I've had to when dealing with the likes of you kids. Now get going so you can be back by dinner. We'll all work together to get Maggie here for the party."

"Yes, ma'am," he said. He saluted then gave her a quick peck on the cheek as he scooped up the truck's keys from the bowl. It felt good to be home.

Jake took Hero with him on the drive to the bookstore. With Oliver napping, Hero seemed restless and eager to spend time with him this afternoon.

The dog loved to ride in the front seat of the truck with his head out the window. Kids in cars passing by loved to wave at him. Occasionally, Hero would draw back into the cab and rub his head against Jake's shoulder. Jake smiled and petted his friend's head.

On the drive, his thoughts drifted back to his conversation with Pastor Luke the other day.

The more he thought about the temporary choir director position at Old Grace Church, the more it appealed to him. He knew he had to give the pastor an answer soon. As for the work on the farm, he could definitely find time for both.

It was only temporary as he was planning on heading back to Kansas before now to find a job this fall. Soon.

Hero suddenly barked.

"Reading my thoughts?" Jake patted his good friend and wished his buddy could offer some advice.

Jake also thought about all the music that poured out of him in the church. It had been a long time since he'd felt that way. It was time to take his guitar out of its case again.

Soon it was mission accomplished with buying Maggie's birthday presents.

After his success at the bookstore, he headed home. He couldn't quite believe how his life had changed. He certainly hadn't envisioned a visit lasting over the summer, which is what this was turning out to be. Or the miracle of forgiveness that was being offered on a daily basis from his family.

Or Oliver being his son. Oliver was finally warming up to him. And he was grateful, pure and simple.

Pulling off the road toward the farm, Jake noticed Oliver sitting on an upside-down bucket by the flower stand

Was Oliver really sitting there...waiting for him? The thought warmed him head to toe.

After making a delivery, Maggie pulled into the driveway. She was blown away by the progress of the flower stand.

There was a small round center piece of stained glass depicting a bouquet of flowers. Maggie had seen it on Gram's bookshelf. Several flower holders adorned the shelves.

It was truly a gorgeous creation.

And there was Oliver "working" with Jake, with Hero there too, of course. Oliver had mentioned watching Jake work a few times. And she took that as a good sign for both of them. She imagined Jake was mighty pleased too.

Oliver looked like he was explaining something about the tools to Hero then delivered them to Jake.

Pulling onto the grass, she cut the ignition and stepped out. The wooden sign was finished and ready to be hung on a rustic wood post. The red lettering really stood out.

This was more than anything Maggie had imagined.

She stepped carefully in case there were tools or nails on the ground. Thankfully, she'd suggested that Oliver wear his boots when out here with Jake.

Jake greeted her. "What do you think? It's coming along, isn't it?"

"It's wonderful. Very eye-catching from the road," she said. "Both of you do good work."

Oliver's eyes grew wide. Wearing rolled-up overalls, he put his thumbs in his pockets like he'd probably seen Jake do a hundred times.

"Glad you l-l-like it, Mom," he said.

"I sure do. You two coming to the birthday party at Gram's? The one I'm not supposed to know anything about?" she asked innocently.

Jake and Oliver suddenly stared at each other as if to say, *I didn't tell her, did you?*

"I'm betting there will be cake and ice cream. You better get cleaned up and ready," she informed her son.

Oliver dropped the screwdriver he was holding and immediately headed toward Maggie. "R-r-ride with you to Gram's?" he asked.

"Better ask your partner there. He may want you to clean the worksite with him," Maggie said.

Oliver suddenly looked worried as if he might be doing something wrong. Maggie wished she hadn't said that.

Jake stepped in quickly. "You put in a good afternoon's work,

Oliver. I'll clean up. You go on ahead. I'm sure Gram and Aunt Zoe need your help."

Oliver slid into the passenger side of her car and buckled up.

Her gaze lingered on Jake. She knew that she was asking a lot of him not to let Oliver know the truth yet. Working side by side daily with Oliver had to be difficult.

Subtly, Jake had let Maggie know he wanted to talk to her about something when she was ready. He'd given her the space she asked for when she told him she had to concentrate on Oliver right now.

They definitely needed to talk. She was sure they both had questions.

It might be her imagination, but the way he looked at her sometimes made her wonder if he might be developing feelings for her again. But he was leaving for Kansas by the end of summer. She needed to protect her heart.

Jake caught her watching him and met her gaze. Sometimes it felt like there was an energy between them that she couldn't describe. Just before Maggie broke eye contact, he gave her an impish wink.

Getting in the car, she couldn't stop smiling. When she looked in the rearview mirror, Jake was still standing in the same spot, with Hero beside him, as he watched her drive away.

At home, Oliver seemed nervous. Maggie thought it might be the anticipation of the party and, of course, cake. His favorite dessert. She wondered what kind Gram had made.

Come to think of it, Oliver had been nervous for a couple days now. She'd been so busy with the business. Maggie felt bad not paying more attention to her own son.

"Mom, can I go to Gram's now?" asked Oliver.

"Let me call first and see if it's all right," said Maggie.

Gram assured Maggie it was fine.

"Yes, you can go. Hero is going to meet you," said Maggie, smiling.

"Oh boy! B-bye, Mom." Oliver gave Maggie a quick peck on the cheek before he ran downstairs.

Today was her birthday, and if she had one deep heartfelt wish, it was that she wanted Oliver feeling better, happier. That would be the best gift possible.

She often wondered how Paul would have dealt with these issues with Oliver. And what it would be like to still have a partner to help with the day-to-day ups and downs.

Paul had always made dinner reservations on her birthday and bought her jewelry. Opening her jewelry box, she admired the gold earrings and her favorite charm bracelet that he had always added a charm to on special occasions. Now she treasured every piece. She fingered the etched primrose locket she'd put on this morning.

So far, it had been a good birthday.

Earlier today, the flower farm crew had gathered inside the office to sing "Happy Birthday." Followed by her blowing out the candles on a long tray of cupcakes decorated with sunflowers.

Zoe had announced that they would soon be launching the newly updated website. Maggie would have to ask Molly to take some photographs of the flower stand and the new sign by the road.

Everyone who worked on the farm had chipped in to give her a gift card with a packet of coupons for the new spa that had opened in Yarmouth. She'd never been to such a place in her life and was looking forward to it.

Sitting in her office, she felt blessed. A knock at the door startled her. It was Zoe.

"Time to collect the birthday girl," she said. Then Zoe added, "You know, the one who knows nada about any party."

Maggie laughed. "Yes, I guess that would be me."

It was hot and muggy as they walked toward Gram's house. Maggie noticed that Zoe slowed down to look at her phone.

"Is everything okay?" she asked.

Zoe shook her head. "I have something I want to show you. I looked up this Pastor Joe friend of Jake's. He had such an impact on my brother's life, I was curious about him."

Maggie had been curious too, but not enough to check out the pastor online.

Zoe held up her phone to show Maggie the church.

"Impressive," Maggie said. Pastor Joe's church was a white modern church with a tall steeple in the middle and a wide glassed-in entrance in the front. The sides fanned out in a half circle as if welcoming people with a hug.

The photos of the church inside showed a wide ring of lights suspended over the pews like a halo. The stained glass window panels were not huge as in some churches but certainly beautiful.

Zoe swiped the screen. "And this is Pastor Joe Carcione. Easy on the eyes, isn't he? I don't know what I was expecting, but it wasn't him."

Handing Maggie the phone again, she told her to swipe right.

Maggie stared at photographs of Jake playing the guitar at church, singing with children gathered around him in Romania, according to the caption. Another photo showed him leading a group of musicians recently in Guatemala City.

There weren't any videos, but the photos were enough to show her the man he'd become. A far cry from all the publicity shots and videos of him rocking out on stage with his band. He'd also become ubiquitous on social media. There had been tons of photos of him signing autographs on tour.

Maggie handed the phone back to her friend.

"I thought it'd be good for us to see the man he is now," Zoe said. "I thought you'd want to know."

Maggie nodded. She asked, "Have you heard him play the guitar since he's been back?"

"Come to think of it, I haven't. What do you make of that?" Zoe asked.

"I don't know. What I do know is here comes Hero to fetch us." Hero bounded toward them, his tongue lolling to one side.

Then Maggie saw Jake and Oliver at the bottom of Gram's porch steps, beckoning them in.

"Hur-ry up, Mom," Oliver called out.

"I think someone is eager for cake," Zoe guessed.

Pleasantly surprised, Maggie was greeted by lights strung around the railing of the stairs to the front porch. Lights were also draped around the front door.

Once inside, Maggie was even more delighted with the pink, blue and yellow balloons.

She loved this family and loved this house. Even more so today, with it all gussied up in party mode.

The yellow kitchen always drew her in like one of Gram's hugs. The warmth of the woodwork. The cheery colors. She knew Gram had sewn all of the curtains herself. The two arched windows let in a lot of light. It felt cheerful even on a cloudy day.

And sitting in the middle of the kitchen table was the largest German chocolate cake she'd ever seen. Striped candles had been placed on top. There were several presents on the kitchen table. She couldn't stop a few tears from sliding down her cheeks.

"It's wonderful," she said.

She felt even more emotional as they sang "Happy Birthday" to her. She saw that Oliver was mesmerized by Jake strumming the guitar.

Even Hero gave her a birthday greeting with a sweet yowl. Everyone laughed. She and her son had definitely developed a soft spot in their hearts for that dog.

The presents were amazing. The leather-bound book on flowers from the nineteenth century was stunning. She was excited about including the flower information on cards along with some of her special orders.

Gram's present was thoughtful as well. Botanical cookbooks. Plus an entire set of flower-shaped pans and cookie cutters. In addition to a flower press for drying flowers.

Gram said, "I love the lavender muffin recipe you created, Maggie."

Maggie blushed.

Jake's gift moved her as well. Weeks ago, she'd mentioned her plans to start hosting weddings at the farm someday. She really hadn't expected him to remember it. He'd gifted her with books on opening wedding venues. Everything from business guides to lovely photobooks full of ideas.

Gram smiled. "When I saw what Jake had bought for you, I thought the flower press might give you some creative ideas. I've seen ornaments with pressed flowers and jewelry. I'd like to learn how too."

"Gram, I'd love that," Maggie gushed. She'd like nothing better than to sit alongside Gram and do some flower projects. Especially during the long winter months.

It felt like everyone around the table got her. They understood who she really was. Yes, they knew she loved flowers and her work on the farm, but this was so much more.

Blowing out the candles on the cake, she wished for wonderful blessings for them all. For her family.

After a wonderful evening, it was getting late and Oliver was fading. Jake offered to help carry all her presents home.

Gram returned to the kitchen from the living room. "I just turned on the TV, and there's a storm warning. You know how these summer storms in Maine can come up out of the blue. This one seems fast moving but due soon. You can stay here if you want or head home. Whichever one you're comfortable with. But if you're going, even though it isn't far, I'd head out now."

Maggie gulped. Oliver didn't like storms and neither did she.

Jake looked at her. "Your call," he said.

"I think we'll head back. Gram, can we use your cart, and I'll return it tomorrow? It'll help with the heavy books."

"Of course, honey. Jake, you're going too, right? Call me when you get there and before you leave, all right?" Gram asked.

"Will do, Gram."

Hero stood beside Oliver and whined.

Gram looked at Jake and nodded toward Oliver, whose hand hadn't left Hero's neck. She spoke up. "What do you think about Hero accompanying you? Zoe and I will be fine here."

Oliver spoke up. "I—I think Hero sh-sh-should come with us. H-he might be a-afraid if we leave wh-when Gram and Aunt Zoe go to bed."

"It's getting dark, they might want to go to bed early. You could be right," said Jake. "What do you think, Hero? Want to come with us?"

Hero stood and shook his body. Then he nudged Oliver toward the door.

"I think Hero says that we're ready to go," said Jake. "The storm is brewing!"

# *Chapter Nine*

As Jake and Hero walked Maggie and Oliver home, Jake noted that Oliver obsessively watched the sky as it grew darker. Hero stayed by his side and nudged his hand from time to time.

Jake attempted to distract Oliver. "What do you think, buddy? Did your mom have a good birthday party? Did we all do all right?"

Oliver nodded. He turned to Maggie. "Mom, I—I wanted to get you a t-tele-telescope for your b-b-birthday." Oliver said. "We c-c-could watch the sky."

Surprised, Maggie responded, "That's an awesome idea, honey. We'll look into that. We could watch the stars and see the phases of the moon up close."

Jake noted she didn't say anything about watching the weather.

A low rumble of thunder sounded off in the distance. Oliver cringed. Hero edged closer to him.

"It's okay, sweetie. It's still a ways off, and we're almost home."

After a few minutes, Jake felt large raindrops hit him just as they made it to the house.

"We all better hurry inside," Maggie urged.

Once they were inside and out of the rain, Oliver double-checked to make sure the door was locked. Jake then watched Oliver take charge of gathering up the birthday presents from the doorway and bringing them into the living room. Hero walked back and forth with him as Oliver took one present at a time with each trip.

"Jake, I know it's not far back to Gram's, but we wouldn't want you to head back with the storm coming in. How about some coffee? Or tea?" Maggie asked.

"Tea would be good, thanks," he said. Jake slid his jacket off and hung it on the coat rack. He had noticed that both Maggie and Oliver took off their shoes and set them on the mat near the front door. He followed suit.

Glancing around, everything looked modern, sleek, polished. Not what he'd expected. Black, white, grays and neutral wood tones dominated the color palette. Overall there was an architectural vibe.

"Did you design this?" he asked her as he entered the kitchen.

"This? No, a designer Gram hired did the work. Someone Zoe knew from college who opened her own business. It was originally intended to be a rental property, which is why it looks like this. It's a nice house."

Jake noted she didn't say home.

It was definitely a far cry from the one-story house that used to be here.

"Quite a change, I know," Maggie said. "It has two stories now. Bedrooms are upstairs with a shared bathroom. Feel free to wander around while I make us tea," she said.

In the living room, Oliver sat in a chair by the window and seemed to be absorbed in a hand-held game. His only break in concentration was to periodically look out the window to check the weather. So far, there was nothing more than rain outside.

Jake wandered around the house, seeing Maggie's touches everywhere. A soft rainbow-colored throw draped over the couch. Fresh flowers in vases. Framed photographs on the walls. Books, books and more books.

He caught sight of a small nook with a wooden desk and

chair tucked into an alcove in the hallway, off the kitchen. The walls were splashed with colorful drawings of garden ideas and magazine cutouts. Stacks of file folders. Loose pens and pencils. Two pots of African violets sat on the windowsill. Definitely Maggie's space. Wandering into the kitchen, he saw impressive stainless-steel appliances. A double oven. A big deep sink. An island in the middle with a granite countertop. Butter-yellow lace curtains. Small paintings on the wall. More vases of flowers.

"Maggie, what would you want in a home if you could design it?" he asked.

She hesitated for a moment. "An extra room for Oliver to spread out in. A room for him to indulge in his interests over time."

"That sounds good. What about you, Maggie? What would you want?"

Maggie closed her eyes. "A library room for my flower and gardening books. Wood shelves and the light streaming in from a tall arched window. And a large wooden table in the middle for researching and planning."

"What else?" Jake prompted.

Maggie smiled, her eyes still closed. "Wide window sills in the kitchen for growing herbs. And a bay window in the living room for a Christmas tree."

Jake watched as she opened her eyes slowly as if she didn't want to leave what she had just envisioned.

"Thank you for sharing that, Maggie," said Jake. The lights blinked briefly. The thunder definitely sounded closer.

Maggie exchanged a look with Jake. Then she sought out Oliver. "Do you want something to eat or drink before bed, honey?" she asked him.

"M-more b-birthday cake?" suggested Oliver as he headed to the kitchen with Hero.

"Really? I suppose a small piece wouldn't hurt before bed.

I wonder if Uncle Jake would like any. Should we share with him?" Maggie asked.

Oliver nodded solemnly.

Jake took that to be a very good sign. Cake was cake, after all.

Maggie and Oliver began setting out plates, forks and knives.

Jake's cell phone vibrated. It was Gram. "Yes, I'll be staying here for a little while. Mags hasn't kicked me out."

"Not yet," Maggie called out.

Jake hung up and said, "Gram saw on the radar..." Maggie immediately shook her head at him.

Jake caught on and stopped what he was saying. They didn't want to frighten Oliver any more than he already was with the approaching storm.

"Have you been playing music since you've been back?" Maggie asked Jake.

"Interesting you asked me that. I recently played the piano at Gram's church. It felt really good."

"I remember," Maggie said, "you started out playing the piano."

Jake took a sip of tea. "That's right."

"Are you still composing music?" she asked.

"Sometimes. Mostly songs of worship."

"M-Mom sings," Oliver injected.

"I do not," said Maggie.

"Yes, y-you, you do. You're off-key a lot b-b-but you sing in the shower all the time," stated Oliver emphatically.

Jake loved seeing Maggie's face turn a deep shade of red.

"Busted," she said. "I do."

"Sometimes sh-sh-she sings your..."

"Oliver!" Maggie interrupted.

Jake was enjoying this conversation way too much.

"Do you like music, Oliver?" Jake asked, trying to give Maggie some breathing room.

"I—I—I write songs," he said. "My t-t-teacher said they're like p-p-poetry, but they're real songs."

"That's great! If you feel like it, I'd love to hear them sometime."

*What's that expression—chip off the old block?* Jake chuckled.

A flash of lightning followed by a deep boom of thunder signaled the storm was getting closer.

To distract Oliver, Maggie spoke up. "So, when is your car going to be fixed, Jake? Have you heard anything?"

"I have. It'll be another week. Matt was away for a while, and there was a delay in getting some parts, apparently." He took a forkful of Gram's wonderful cake.

"When are you leaving for Kansas?" she asked, looking down at her plate.

It was a question Jake wasn't ready for. Before he could swallow his cake to answer, Oliver erupted.

"What?" Oliver shouted. "You're l-l-leaving? It's all my f-f-fault, isn't it? He's mad at me." Clearly overwrought, Oliver leapt out of his chair and ran for the stairs, Hero at his heels.

"Oliver! Wait!" Maggie went after him. "Come back!"

Jake stood up suddenly. The lights blinked again. And then, everything went black.

He tried to follow Maggie in the dark. He was at a disadvantage not being familiar with the layout of the house.

*Where are the stairs?*

His heartbeat accelerated. He listened for the sound of footsteps.

Thankfully, there was a flash of lightning. He caught a glimpse of Maggie, and he headed in the right direction.

At the top of the stairs, Maggie grabbed a flashlight off a hall table and ran into a room.

Jake followed closely behind her.

The storm was on top of them. The wind blew hard. Rain pelted the windows.

Maggie turned on the flashlight and handed it to him as she sat on Oliver's bed.

He directed the light toward the ceiling. Oliver rocked on the bed as he gripped his pillow tightly.

"Oliver, honey, can you tell me what's wrong?" Maggie pleaded.

Oliver looked up at his mother then Jake, then lowered his head into his pillow. The only sound was muffled sobs.

Eventually he lifted his head and spoke. "T-t-tell me the truth?" he asked.

"Always," Maggie said. "You have to tell me what is going on, Oliver. Please, honey."

Hero nudged Oliver. Jake hadn't been aware of Hero entering the room but was glad he was there.

Oliver sat up but still rocked continuously. Jake's heart thumped fast; he didn't know what to do.

"D-d-did I cause the car accident s-s-somehow?" Oliver managed to ask before sobbing.

"What? No, honey," said Maggie in disbelief. "A semi lost control, and there were several cars involved in the crash."

"I—I don't re-re-member anything. I remember someone said I was in the car." Oliver twisted his pillow and sobbed.

"I know you don't remember, honey. An ambulance brought you to the hospital. And I met you there." Jake saw Maggie tremble as she spoke about that day.

Bewildered, Maggie looked at Jake. Then she asked Oliver gently, "Is that why you think Jake is mad at you?"

Oliver nodded. "I—I—I didn't know. I—I—I can't remember."

Heart pounding, Jake spoke up in a shaky voice. "Oliver, you had nothing to do with what happened. Like your mom said, it was an accident. We all miss Paul, but we are all so thankful you're still here. We love you, Oliver, so much."

Jake didn't know what else to say. He hoped it was enough.

Suddenly, he saw Oliver's hand reach out in his direction.

He sat down on the bed next to him, and Oliver's hand clutched his shirt. Jake laid the flashlight on the bed and put his arms around both Oliver and Maggie.

Maggie couldn't believe that Oliver had been carrying around all this fear and guilt. He thought that he had been somehow responsible for Paul's death? And that Jake was perhaps holding it against him? Her heart shattered just thinking about it.

Maggie heard Oliver take a deep breath when Jake sat down on the bed with them. She was so grateful for Jake being there.

Maggie noticed Hero on the other side of him, his head on Oliver's lap.

The room was dark except for the stream of light from the flashlight pointed toward the ceiling.

The three of them sat huddled together. Oliver continued sobbing softly.

Jake smoothed the top of Oliver's head. Maggie knew he had to feel the scar that was there.

She looked at Jake just as he leaned forward to briefly rest his cheek against hers. It was that tender gesture that gave her strength.

But she feared it wasn't the end of learning what fears burdened their son.

As Oliver shook a bit less, Maggie bravely asked, "Honey, do you have any other questions?"

There was another boom of thunder as Oliver ducked down closer and nodded yes. She felt Jake hold them closer.

*Keep me strong,* Maggie prayed.

"D-d-did I cause the f-f-fire?" Oliver asked as he started to shake again.

"No. No. You did not. It started up the block," Maggie said.

"Are y-you sure?" Oliver asked between sobs.

Maggie felt Jake gently rub her sweat-soaked back.

"Honey, I know you don't remember the fire. I read the report to you from the fire department," Maggie gently reminded her son.

"O-okay," said Oliver.

Shivers ran down Maggie's spine as all the memories of the fire came roaring back. Followed by her fears about Oliver. The endless rounds of waiting rooms, scans, tests and doctors. She had tried hard not to think of the worst case scenario. And she prayed and prayed. The realization came of all they had been through and survived. She knew she could deal with whatever came next.

In the faint light of the flashlight, Maggie saw Oliver's wet, blotchy face. Oliver wiped his nose on his pajama sleeve.

"You were so brave, Oliver. You called out so the fireman could come find us," Maggie said.

She reached out to her son and wiped some of his tears off his cheeks.

A heaviness permeated the moment.

Oliver stopped rocking and hugged his pillow tighter.

"Do you have any more questions?" Maggie asked. She held her breath, waiting. She felt Jake do the same.

Oliver shook his head.

The storm inside and outside seemed to be passing.

Oliver straightened. His voice cracked as he admitted, "I—I was j-j-just so afraid and m-mad and s-sad b-because I—I didn't know."

Maggie cupped his small face with her hand. "You can always ask me anything. Anytime. Or Gram or Aunt Zoe or Uncle Jake. Okay?"

Oliver nodded, then his eyes widened. "I—I'm sorry, Mom. I spoiled your b-b-birthday."

Maggie's heart flipped. "No, you didn't, honey. No way. You are my best present ever. And now that I know what you've been worried about, I love you even more."

The three of them huddled together a bit longer until Oliver started to hiccup. Maggie smiled; he always laughed when he got the hiccups.

And sure enough…of everything possible during this tumultuous night, Oliver giggled.

Then Oliver hiccupped again. Jake chuckled. He put up his hand for a high five, and Oliver slapped it in response.

Then the three of them broke the huddle. They laughed in sheer and utter relief from all the emotions.

Even Hero's yowl was a cause for laughter.

Though Maggie's head pounded, she felt lighter.

"Feeling better, buddy?" Jake asked.

Oliver nodded and yawned. He rubbed his eyes and leaned back on the bed.

"Do you think you can get some sleep now, honey?" Maggie asked.

Clearly exhausted, eyes heavy with fatigue, he slowly fell back on his other pillow. Hero edged closer so Oliver could reach him.

Maggie and Jake got up from the bed.

All the turmoil seemed to have evaporated.

"I think it's best if we just let him sleep." Maggie picked up a folded blanket at the foot of the bed. Then pulled it up to cover her son.

Jake picked up the flashlight, pointed the light toward the floor, then they exited the room slowly.

Maggie saw Hero lift his head. Jake commanded, "Stay."

Out in the hall, Jake caught Maggie's arm to steady her as she stumbled from sheer exhaustion.

"Mags, I think you need to go to bed too," he cautioned.

She nodded.

All her emotions and thoughts were tripping over one another. She was truly crashing after the rush of adrenaline. It had been heartbreaking hearing her son's painful revelations.

"I'll see you out," she said.

"No, please don't," Jake said. "I'll stay a little longer downstairs then let myself out. The batteries in the flashlight are working fine, so I can see. I think it's best if Hero stays tonight in Oliver's room."

"Okay. Jake, I—"

"Shh, Mags, we'll talk soon. And don't worry about tomorrow. I'll let Zoe know, and we'll take care of the flower business. Will you let me...let us help?"

She searched Jake's face but wasn't sure what she was looking for before she agreed.

He reached out for her. She leaned into his arms and buried her face against his neck. "Thank you for everything. Good night, Jake," she said softly as she stepped back.

"Good night, Mags. Until tomorrow then. Try to get some sleep."

She went back upstairs, flipped the light switch in her bedroom without registering that the electricity had come back on and softly closed the door, leaving it slightly ajar.

Before she went to bed though, she tiptoed back to Oliver's room and listened. Thankfully, she heard only Hero's snoring.

At five in the morning, Maggie jerked awake at the sound of someone accidently knocking over the coat rack followed by the front door opening and closing.

Peering out the window, she saw the sun's first rays rise above the horizon. She saw tree branches scattered across the yard from last night's storm.

Then she saw Jake headed back toward Gram's house. He must have slept on the couch downstairs all night. She felt truly grateful.

And today, she knew that Jake would let Gram and Zoe know about Oliver's breakthrough.

And the flower farm business would be fine without her for the day. She knew she'd be kept in the loop if she was needed. There was a delivery today, but Zoe could handle it.

She had no idea what the day would bring. She hoped what happened last night with her son was a breakthrough.

*Please God. Let it be so.*

She watched Jake until she couldn't see him anymore. She put her hand over the heart that she needed to protect.

# Chapter Ten

At his request, Maggie and Gram gave Jake several photo albums. Jake pored over them hungrily, looking for photos of Oliver. He wanted to memorize everything he could from his son's life that he'd missed up to that point.

Three days later after the storm, Jake wondered if there would be a new normal for everyone after Oliver's recent breakthrough. He also wondered about Oliver's quietness, if it was partly due to shyness.

Oliver's social skills were improving. The bus driver that picked the kids up for camp mentioned that Oliver no longer sat in the front near him but in the back with the other kids. It sounded like the driver almost missed Oliver's company, though he was very happy Oliver was interacting with others more.

Jake hoped Oliver's confidence level would improve. He was clearly happy working with Jake on projects. Jake had made a small plaque for the flower stand, stating that he and Oliver had built it. Jake smiled whenever he saw Oliver polishing it with his sleeve.

Zoe often kidded Jake in private that Oliver was his mini-me.

Just then, Jake saw his phone ring.

"Jake, you're not going to believe it," Maggie said, clearly excited and a little breathless.

"Try me," he said.

"A reporter from *The Sweet Springs Gazette* saw the new

sign and flower stand that you and Oliver built. She called and came out this morning for an interview. A photographer accompanied her and made sure that every member of the farm crew working today was included in the shots. Not only that, but Oliver and Hero are in one of the photos!" Maggie said.

"That's wonderful, Maggie." Jake couldn't be happier.

"I'm definitely going to frame the article and put it on the office wall," Maggie declared.

"You really should," said Jake.

"I have to run. Just wanted to share the news," Maggie said.

"Thank you so much for telling me, Maggie. I'm really excited for you and everyone on the farm," Jake told her.

Sitting back, he smiled to himself. The flower stand by the road had only been open to the public a few days. He knew it had already been bringing in extra revenue. All of Maggie's employees had a hand in putting together the bouquets and displays for the stand. There was talk of an ongoing competition for who sold the most bouquets each week.

Jake's next project for Maggie's business was even bigger. He had to consult with Matt when he picked up his car from the garage. He wondered how well Oliver could keep a secret from his mother. It would be good to have his help and would mean so much to Maggie.

Maybe on his way into town, he'd stop by the church and ask the pastor a few questions about the choir director position. The more he thought about it, the more he was intrigued and excited about it.

Maybe he should ask Maggie to go to town with him. It made sense, since he needed to pick up his car and drive it back to Gram's. They could have lunch together. Visit Dairy Moo for a treat and sit in the park together. Like a real date.

Jake was certain that Maggie was happy about Oliver's progress. But even with Oliver's revelation and hopeful improvement, Jake was concerned about Maggie. She still seemed exhausted.

He remembered Zoe saying that Maggie hadn't used any of the spa coupons from her birthday gift yet. It had only been three very busy days but maybe he should encourage her to do that. She juggled more and more must-dos on any given day.

Maggie had already given two of the coupons away. Yesterday, she wrapped a bouquet of flowers from her special garden and included the coupons as a thank-you for their neighbor Carly, the PA, for when she came over that night and checked out Oliver and Hero.

Some days, he couldn't imagine not seeing Maggie and Oliver on a daily basis. He had to admit it, plain and simple, Jake wanted more of a relationship with Maggie. So much so, he often caught himself praying, *Keep me patient, Lord.*

His phone vibrated. Zoe wanted to meet at the office. It was time to put the plan in motion of taking Maggie to town.

Whistling as he arrived at the office, he found Oliver and Hero sitting with Zoe and Maggie.

Jake smiled. "I heard *The Sweet Springs Gazette* was here and everyone had their pictures taken today?" Jake said.

"I-it was l-like at school," Oliver said.

"Pretty cool, I bet," said Jake.

Oliver nodded then said, "J-Jake, knock-knock."

"Hmm," Jake said. "Who's there?"

"Spell," Oliver said.

"Spell who," replied Jake.

"Okay, w-h-o," said Oliver.

Everyone laughed, and they high-fived Oliver.

Maggie, clearly astonished, said, "Oliver, you just made a joke!"

Jake noticed that Oliver joked almost without stuttering but didn't want to call attention to it.

A few moments later, Oliver and Hero headed off to the

greenhouse with Amy. She always seemed to enjoy when they showed up, even when she had work to do.

Zoe told him that she had numerous calls to make and went to her office, leaving Jake and Maggie alone.

"Since we're alone, mind if I ask you something personal?" Maggie asked Jake.

"Go ahead, Mags," said Jake.

"Just a sec," She got up and took two bottled waters out of the dorm-size refrigerator.

When she sat down again, she asked, "So, what was it like to be a member of the country rock group No Caution?" she asked.

That took Jake by surprise. He didn't realize that Maggie was interested in hearing about his past. He unscrewed the cap of the water bottle and took a long drink before answering her.

"Good for the most part," Jake said. "My bandmates and I all worked well together. Sure, there were some skirmishes and creative disputes, but mostly we stuck together." He gave a faint smile. "We're all still friends and stay in touch."

"Why did you leave the band?" asked Maggie. "I've always wanted to know."

He drummed his fingers on the table. He'd been asked this same question by fans and reporters over the years.

"I finally realized that it wasn't the kind of music I most wanted to make." Jake couldn't—wouldn't—mention the heartbreak he felt when he'd heard about her marriage to Paul.

"Sounds like it was a difficult time for you," said Maggie.

"Yeah, my feelings were all over the place. I couldn't turn them off like a spigot. I was a rock star hitting rock bottom," Jake said. "When I left, the press tried to get me to talk. And when they couldn't, they invented reasons. Paparazzi followed me until I ended up in Kansas by chance and quite literally changed my life by walking into a church and falling asleep on a pew."

Maggie's eyes grew wide. "Have you thought about telling your story? You can set the record straight."

Jake smiled. "I don't need to. As long as God and my family understand, I'm good. I'll do it if it helps someone. Now, I write the music I want to write. I'm grateful every day for Pastor Joe, who woke me up, literally, the morning after I fell asleep on that pew."

She leaned back and took a drink of water. "I'm happy and so proud of you, Jake."

Her acceptance was healing, and he let it wash over him.

When he looked at her, she was illuminated by the light from the window. His heart sped up.

"Thank you, Jake, for sharing that part of your life with me."

"My pleasure," Jake said, realizing he meant it.

"I'm glad things didn't get busy while we were talking," said Maggie.

Jake nodded. It had been a gift to talk to Maggie about something that he didn't let himself think about very often.

Reaching over, she touched his arm.

"Thank you, Maggie. Me too. I'm a work in progress every day."

Maggie smiled warmly. "We all are, Jake. We all are."

Suddenly, the door opened. Oliver, Hero and Gloria walked in with a box of muffins.

"Wow! You found those in the greenhouse? You really have great green thumbs!" said Maggie as she reached for a blueberry muffin.

"No, that would be me who brought them," said Dee Dee, one of Maggie's favorite customers, who walked in behind them. Jake had met Dee Dee a couple times. She was an actress who performed over the years at the Ogunquit Playhouse about an hour south along the coast. Looking at her, she certainly had a theatrical style of clothing and hair color. Today it looked like her color choices were orange and purple.

Maggie asked, "How can we help you today?"

Dee Dee waved a piece of paper in the air. "I have a list with me. Things I'd like. Well, if you can help me find them really."

"Happy to help." Maggie walked around her desk to greet her.

But before she left, she said, "Jake, thank you again for sharing."

It was a now or never moment. Jake hadn't had a chance to ask Maggie about tomorrow.

He cleared his throat.

"I'm going into town tomorrow to run some errands and pick up the car. I was wondering, Mags, if you could drive in with me? You could play hooky from work. Maybe shop, use one of the spa coupons? Then we could meet up and grab some lunch?" he suggested.

"She'd be happy to. I can cover for her," Zoe chimed in.

Everyone in the office laughed.

"Looks like it's a yes then," said Maggie.

Jake smiled at the pink in her cheeks.

Maggie didn't need to turn around to know Jake was watching her as she walked away. She couldn't help but grin.

Dee Dee fanned herself as she hurried along beside Maggie.

"My word, if a man looked at me the way that man looks at you, I'd melt," she declared. "Is he your new boyfriend?" she asked. "If not, he should be."

"It's complicated. He's back home for a visit and helping out on the farm. He's trying to catch up with his family."

"I'd say he's trying to date you, as well," Dee Dee said, still fanning herself and looking back at the office dramatically.

Maggie felt her cheeks flush then held out her hand. "Let's look at that list, shall we?"

After Maggie helped Dee Dee, things got busy, with customers coming in nonstop for several hours.

Helping people find the perfect flowers was often like being a therapist. People came in with stories of why they wanted flowers for themselves or for others. She'd had several customers like that today.

One little neighbor girl came over to buy flowers to cheer her mother up because she lost a promotion at work. When she saw the sunflowers, she pointed and said, "Oh, those please!" Maggie wrapped a few of them up with sunflower paper and a big yellow bow.

But her very best customer was Nate, a middle-aged gentleman who had been coming in a couple times a week this past month to buy flowers. He was gathering up the courage to propose marriage to his girlfriend. He struggled every day to choose just the right flower to say just the right thing. He always ended up asking Maggie for help.

Nate and Maggie would consult the flower lore book that Zoe and Oliver gave her for her birthday. Then she designed a little 4x4 inch card with the meaning and a little drawing to go along with the flower he picked each day.

Today, he returned with his fiancée, Louise, a lovely, demure woman with round glasses, her long dark hair swept up in a bun. She wanted to meet Maggie.

Louise showed Maggie her antique solitaire diamond ring with a white gold band, which had been Nate's mother's.

Then Louise held up a beautifully carved frame that held all the cards with Maggie's drawings and flower meanings on them.

"I saved every one," Louise said, a slight catch in her voice.

Maggie held her hand to her heart. "Louise, that's beautiful. Nate is a real treasure."

"You're a treasure too, Maggie. This is all so above and beyond. Thank you!" gushed Louise.

A little teary-eyed, both women hugged one another.

"Have you set a date for the wedding yet?" Maggie asked.

Nate cleared his throat and looked at Louise. "We'd love to get married in early September. The sooner the better, but we know that's probably impossible."

Maggie didn't need to ask if they meant *this* year. And yes, it was very soon, a month away.

On impulse, Maggie said, "What about getting married here at the farm?"

More than a little bit shocked, Louise asked, "Are you serious?"

"I am," said Maggie. "Full disclosure, you'd be our first wedding here, and the time frame—well, I can't do super fancy."

"That's fine! It's so beautiful here," gushed Nate.

"I agree," said Louise as she linked arms with her fiancé.

"And think about it, all your courting flowers have come from here," said Maggie.

Nate blushed.

"What do you say? Of course take time to think about it," said Maggie.

Nate and Louise looked at each other. They nodded then spoke at the same time: "Let's do it!"

"Wonderful! It's set then," declared Maggie. "Decide on the date, and we'll get started planning."

Maggie felt like a thousand butterflies were fluttering inside her. Her wedding venue business was beginning.

She was totally excited…and scared out of her wits. Could she actually pull this off?

Later when Maggie had a moment to herself at home, she prayed. *Lord, I felt You with me today.*

She knew there was so much to plan. But for now, she wanted to cherish the moment.

She truly loved everything about her life with flowers.

Her thoughts drifted to Jake. Lunch tomorrow. Like a…date.

Oliver would be with Gram and Zoe. Jake had errands. And what was *she* going to do tomorrow? A whole day in town.

Her mind wandered. There'd been so much change this summer.

Oliver and Jake. They were clearly bonding. Her son enjoyed Jake's company.

And he enjoyed Hero's company as well. Having the sweet dog in his life, Oliver was so much less moody and anxious overall.

She kept thanks flowing heavenward for the progress.

Thinking about tomorrow, she looked in the mirror and realized that her hair hadn't really been touched in years. Back in North Carolina, she'd been faithful about her hair salon appointments. She'd always kept her hair trimmed and styled. Now it had grown out, and if she thought about it at all, she swept it away from her face into a ponytail. She could visit Mary at Chic and Sleek Salon and make an appointment for another day. Or maybe call to see if there were any cancellations.

Now she was getting into thinking of this as a self-care day. What did Zoe say to do? Pamper herself.

Seeing Oliver's changes, she felt she could ease her worrying a bit.

Who was she now? She felt she was mixing the old Maggie with the new Maggie.

Jake had mentioned possibly lunch then the park.

Maggie asked him more than once for a list of expenses for supplies and labor for the beautiful flower stand and new sign by the road, and he had adamantly refused. She could offer to treat him to lunch. But where? Silly question. His favorite place, the Wild Onion Diner.

Maggie went to the fridge and rummaged around the bottom drawer until she found what she hoped was a juicy mandarin orange. She grabbed a napkin and headed outside to the rocking chair on the porch to continue her plotting.

Suddenly, she was surprised by Hero, his feet stepping on

the wooden floor. She ruffled his ears then stood up to check out who came with him. No one.

"Wait here," she told him. Hero promptly sat down by her chair. When she turned to look at him from the doorway, she could see that he would be waiting and watching intently for her return. Maggie had taken to buying dog biscuits since Hero visited Oliver so often lately. She also found a bowl to give him some water.

Sitting with Hero brought her a peaceful feeling. It seemed she was always worrying about something related to the business or Oliver. A moment in the rocking chair with a sweet dog by her side munching dog biscuits was just about perfect.

"So, what do you think I should do tomorrow, Hero? Treat myself?"

"Woof," answered Hero, who then plopped down and promptly started to snore.

Maggie joined him in a nap until a text from Zoe woke her up.

You'll want to check over the inventory tomorrow.

Any problems?

Just some questions about changes being suggested by a couple suppliers due to time constraints and shipping concerns.

All right. BTW, I booked our first wedding next month.

?????

Maggie's phone rang immediately.

"Next month? This September?" asked Zoe incredulously.

"Yes," said Maggie, who couldn't help smiling. She knew Zoe was probably *not* smiling.

"Maggie Madison, what did you do?" asked Zoe in a high-pitched voice.

"You remember Nate? That nice man who has been buying flowers for his now fiancée, Louise? They booked their wedding with us. I told him it would be our first wedding." Maggie grinned.

"I take it that it was your suggestion? We aren't at all ready, and weddings take a lot of planning. I am happy to hear that he finally popped the question though."

"Right? I know. Me too! And I just had this strong feeling to ask them about it. Gram always says, 'When the time is right, the Lord will make it happen.'"

Zoe sighed deeply. "You sound just like her—and my brother."

Maggie wished she was telling Zoe in person. A while ago, they were both lapsed believers together. Zoe had been a believer growing up, but she hadn't returned. She'd never really discussed why.

As for Maggie, she'd had a hard time believing when everything was so overwhelming. She thought when she needed Him most, she felt He wasn't there. But then in quiet moments, she felt Him there drawing her close. And she began opening herself up slowly.

"It'll be an adventure," Maggie said enthusiastically. She hoped Zoe would be able to get on board and feel the same.

"Oh, it will be, all right," Zoe agreed. "It will be. Have fun in town tomorrow with my brother."

"I'll try," said Maggie as she felt a few butterflies in her stomach just at the thought of spending time with Jake.

"This wedding, Maggie, is kind of out of character for you," Zoe said softly.

Maggie laughed. "Are you saying because I didn't overthink

it, make lists, endlessly weigh the pros and cons and I jumped in with both feet?"

"Exactly!" Zoe said.

"You're right," said Maggie then added, "it feels good."

"That's all I need to hear. Good enough for me. Let's do our first Maggie's Flower Farm wedding!" Zoe said.

"Thank you. Thank you for everything, Zoe. I don't think I say that often enough."

# Chapter Eleven

The next day was shaping up to be a busy one. First, Jake had an appointment with Pastor Luke to discuss the job with the church choir. Then he was spending the day with Maggie.

Heading downstairs, he found Gram in the kitchen. She poured two coffees and put them down on the table when he arrived. Something was clearly on her mind.

"Jake, we need to talk about your father," she began.

Jake felt his insides immediately tense up. "He deserted the three of us and left us to fend for ourselves. If you hadn't taken us in, I don't know what would have happened. I'll always be grateful to you for that, Gram."

"There's no doubt that you've all been the light of my life. But what you think happened regarding your father is not quite what happened. Your father did return," Gram said.

Jake was silent. What did Gram mean? He didn't have any memories of seeing his father again.

Gram continued, "Your father was a shell of himself when your mother died. He left. But he eventually returned to the house and found all of you kids had disappeared."

"Our old apartment?" Jake asked.

"Yes, another family had moved in. He was determined to learn where you all were. A neighbor finally told him that I had taken you all in. He came here and told me that he was sorry, then left abruptly."

Jake was surprised to learn this. "It doesn't change things much. He still abandoned his children," he said.

"True," said Gram sadly. "And Zoe and Paul had nightmares for a long time about your father's desertion after your mother died."

Regret stabbed him a thousandfold. Had he done the same thing to them when he'd left?

Gram gripped her coffee cup.

"I hired a private investigator years ago and came up empty," Jake said.

"So did I," Gram said. "Not a trace of him."

Jake remembered Maggie mentioning Paul had also searched for their father, to no avail.

"I sometimes wonder if he's even still alive, Gram," said Jake.

Gram got up from the table and came back with her Bible. She pulled out a grainy newspaper photo of a man taken in a crowd at a rodeo event several years ago. His father was unmistakable. It was taken in Oklahoma, just south of Kansas, where Jake had been living.

Jake couldn't wrap his head around it.

"Did you show this to Zoe or Paul?" asked Jake.

Gram shook her head. She got up, kissed Jake on the top of his head, then headed to her bedroom and shut the door softly behind her.

He sat there. What was he feeling right now? Was his father possibly alive? That news seemed momentous. Jake needed time to process everything, to chat with God about it. Not now though.

He had to pick up Maggie. He knew the camp bus had already picked up Oliver for the day.

He checked his phone again after his talk with Gram. Mags hadn't called to cancel, which was a good sign.

"You clean up pretty good," said Maggie appreciatively as she handed him some boxes for the back of his truck. It did funny things to his insides. No way he'd admit that he changed his clothes more than once this morning.

"You look pretty good yourself, Mags." He took off his hat, slid his sunglasses up and opened the door for her.

"Chivalry is not dead. Good to know," she said.

He was used to seeing her in jeans or overalls and rubber boots on the farm. Today, Maggie was wearing a blue blouse that emphasized the blue in her eyes. She wore tailored slacks and flat shoes that resembled ballet slippers. Her hair was in the ponytail that she often wore. And her perfume smelled flowery, which flower he couldn't say, but it was definitely intoxicating.

Heading out, he tooted the horn twice for Zoe as they drove past the office.

His spirits were high even after the conversation with Gram this morning.

Jake could tell the moment Maggie started to relax. She set her bag down on the seat between them and leaned her elbow on the frame of the open window.

"So, I hear you booked a wedding," he said with a grin.

She laughed. "Oh, I bet you heard a lot about that. How is Zoe feeling about it? Or do I dare ask?" Maggie grinned.

"I'd say she's finally getting over the shock and is in the beginning of the 'excited-about-it' stage," Jake said as he signaled and turned onto the highway.

"Good to know. I'm thrilled and scared. Also very grateful that you bought those books for my birthday. I need to read them pronto!" she said with a smile.

Jake laughed. "Let's not remind Zoe of that birthday present for a day or two, okay? Let's not connect my gift of books on wedding planning with the fact there is now going to be an actual first wedding."

"Chicken," Maggie teased.

"Oliver seems to be doing well lately," Jake said, hoping it was a good time to bring it up.

"Yes," she said simply.

"He just seems brighter in spirit, lighter," Jake said. "And did you notice that he told us a whole joke the other day and barely stuttered?"

"He did? How did I miss that? That's fantastic," Maggie said.

"I didn't want to call attention to it at the time in front of others," he said.

"I think you made the right decision there, Jake. You're good with him. You're..." She hesitated. "You're a good father."

"Thank you, Mags. That means the world to me that you'd say that."

It was quiet in the truck cab for a few minutes.

"Mags?"

"Yes?"

"You mean the world to me too. I'd like to get to know who you are now, if you'll let me." Jake's hands held on to the steering wheel. He wanted to touch her hand but held back. *Patience,* he told himself.

An uncomfortable silence followed.

"Jake," she said and stopped. "I'd like that too, but you're leaving town soon. You're picking your car up today. And we're just getting to know each other again."

He knew he had to tread carefully.

"Yes, and I'm grateful for that. It's more than I deserve. Let's just say, I don't know what my future plans are right now," Jake said as he stopped himself from nervously tapping his fingers on the steering wheel. He glanced at her. She was smiling and looking out the window. That was a positive sign. Words would be nice. But he'd take that smile.

"I think we could proceed slowly," Maggie said quietly.

Jake laughed. "At least you didn't say 'with caution.'"

"I should since the name of your band was No Caution," Maggie joked.

Jake chuckled.

Maggie continued, "We're such different people than we were eleven years ago. A lot has happened to both of us."

He saw her rub the scar on her arm.

"I think we'd need to set some ground rules," Maggie said as she fidgeted beside him.

"Ground rules?"

"I don't like talking about the past," she said simply.

"At all?" Jake asked. "Because getting beyond the hurt and seeing it wasn't *all* bad can be healing. I've found some of the past is certainly worth remembering. It's shaped who we are today. Maybe you could let me help you remember some of the good times?"

There was more silence before Maggie responded. "We could get to know the people we are now and see how it goes. Take it slow. Would you be okay with that?"

Jake's heartbeat was a wild drum solo. "Yes, I'm definitely okay with that. Whatever you feel comfortable with. It's your call," he said.

"Okay, great," she said.

Soon he was pulling into a parking spot by the town hall. She was still smiling.

Before they got out of the pickup, Maggie told him the list of places she needed to go. Then they agreed on a time to meet at the Wild Onion Diner later.

Jake had a special project in mind that he wasn't sharing with her, yet. One that was pretty crucial because of the wedding she'd just agreed to host at the farm. He hoped he'd be able to pull it off in time.

First things first, he had some questions to ask a certain pastor.

* * *

Inside Pastor Luke's office, Jake settled in a comfortable brown leather chair with a high back. The bookshelves and plants gave it a homey feel. Pastor Luke offered Jake a cup of coffee before he quickly glanced over his resume.

"Impressive," said the pastor. "You have a varied musical background. Studies in music theory and vocal technique. And I know you play the piano, which would be a real benefit to the choir."

Jake smiled.

Pastor Luke went on to describe the choir job. They were looking to hire someone full-time in the fall. The previous choir director had met with the choir to rehearse once or twice a week to prepare for Sunday services. In the summer, there were between two to five singers in the choir on a good day.

"On a good day?" Jake asked.

"Yes, people are busy in the summer."

"I see," said Jake.

"Some even have decent voices. I think the Sunday services are enlivened with the choir's participation. And the congregation enjoys them," Pastor Luke said.

However, as he described the times he'd dropped in on rehearsals, he frowned. He said they often had a chaotic feel.

Jake tried to keep his expression neutral. He had a good many questions that weren't being answered yet.

Everything Pastor Luke had described about this job was not what he expected. He might have a better chance of climbing Mount Katahdin in a blizzard than turning this group into a cohesive, focused choir.

"Do you have any questions, Jake?" the pastor asked.

Jake nodded. "Does the choir have a mission statement?"

"I know they should. But we've never had one. It's something I'd very much like to work on with the director though. Perhaps you could create one, then it could be amended with the new director in the fall?" suggested the pastor.

"Yes, that's possible. I'd want it to align with the church's mission, of course," Jake said.

Pastor Luke nodded his head, looking thoughtful.

Jake leaned forward. "How does the choir engage with members of the church as well as the community?"

"They sing on Sundays," Pastor Luke said.

"Hmm, I was just wondering if they engage with the community as a faith-based team for fellowship. Perhaps to draw new members into the church?" Jake suggested.

Pastor Luke shook his head. "No, but that's something I'd certainly approve of. I must say that the questions you've asked are certainly thought-provoking. Let me say here and now that I'm already impressed."

Jake blinked several times.

Pastor Luke chuckled. "Let's show you the rehearsal room."

As they entered, Jake noticed the peeling beige paint on the walls. Part of it was clearly being used as a storage room. There was a small upright piano. Having the two windows open would certainly improve the smell.

"I know it doesn't look like much. No one cared to do anything with it before now," said Pastor Luke as he looked around. "We could certainly clear it out for you."

Jake could envision it with a fresh coat of paint. Maybe a table and chairs for hanging out before practice. Some of Maggie's flowers. A large bulletin board with schedules and events listed.

"So, would you like the job, Jake?" Pastor Luke asked.

He'd worked on missionary assignments with far less resources. With God anything could be accomplished.

Surprising himself, he answered, "Yes, I'd like to take the job."

Pastor Luke shook his hand enthusiastically. "Good! Good! We'll get this room cleaned out for you, except for the piano, of course. You do what you like with the space, and I'll contact the choir members. What day do you want them here?"

"Tuesday afternoon at six p.m. See how that works for them, and we can move to seven p.m. if it conflicts with dinner times.

Let me know if there are problems," said Jake. "And thank you for the job."

"Thank *you*, Jake! Happy to have you on board," said Pastor Luke as they walked back to the office.

When Jake stepped out into the bright sunshine, he wasn't totally convinced that he hadn't lost his mind. But he was smiling, so that was good.

He headed to Matt's garage to see about his car.

When Matt entered his waiting room, he saw Jake arms crossed and looking at the ceiling. He asked him, "Are you all right?"

"Think so," said Jake as he stood up to settle the bill at the desk. "Thank you, Matt. I'll be back later today to pick up the car, though. I'm meeting Maggie first."

Jake got out his wallet to pay Matt a second time.

Matt shook his head. "Are you sure you're all right, my friend? Let's take a break," Matt decided and grabbed two cups of coffee from his office before showing Jake around back. They sat at a picnic table behind the garage.

Jake took a long swig of coffee. It was strong and black.

"So, what's up, Jake?" Matt asked.

"Know where I could get a horse and buggy around here?" he asked.

"What? Horse and buggy?" Matt looked befuddled.

"Yup. I have a favor to ask, man. If you have the time." Jake spelled out his plan to surprise Maggie with a kind of Cinderella-type carriage. And that it needed to be here before a wedding in September that Maggie had agreed to have at the farm.

"Tall order but sounds like a challenge. I like a challenge," said Matt.

That was music to Jake's ears.

Maggie hadn't seen her hairdresser, Mary Ricci, since last Christmas when they'd worked together raising money for the children's wing at Sweet Springs Medical Center. Mary's hair was shorter and red, not blond. And she was glowing. She held out her hand and Maggie noticed a beautiful oval-cut diamond engagement ring.

"Stu asked me this past weekend. We're planning on a long engagement but I don't know if I can wait!" Mary laughed.

"I'm so happy for you!" exclaimed Maggie.

"Thank you! I don't think my feet have touched the ground since he asked me," Mary said.

"I understand," Maggie said. "I want to thank you for getting me in so quickly."

"I had a cancellation and it worked out well, didn't it? What are you thinking? Do you want highlights?" Mary asked Maggie as she pulled out Maggie's hair from the ponytail. "Your hair is such a lovely chestnut brown, I don't know that you need them," she mused.

Sitting in the chair at the salon, Maggie was indecisive. "I don't think I'm ready for highlights. I'm thinking mid-length and something easier to maintain."

"Got it. Relax. You're in my hands," Mary said.

An hour later, she was pleased with the result. It was a below the jawline bob cut. The hairdo was fun and flirty.

"I love it," she told Mary and gave her what she hoped was a generous tip. "A flower bouquet is on me when you come out to the farm!"

Mary hugged her and then went to welcome the next client into her chair.

Walking up the street, Maggie caught sight of herself in a store window and was surprised. She didn't recognize herself.

Focusing back on the matter at hand, Maggie thought that she'd try to source as many local businesses as she could for the wedding venue.

Next, she had an appointment with the Mainely Gatherings to price chairs and tables. They had all the ribbons and sashes she wanted as well. She could put small vases with flowers at the ends of the aisles. She said she'd get back to them about the lighting. All in all, it was a successful appointment.

At the craft store, she picked up what she needed for the boutonnieres, corsages and wristlets. There were also flower crowns to be made.

Maggie was grateful that the bride to be, Louise, was so excited to help and said her wedding party was on board as well.

Maggie felt so blessed, She was relieved that this was a laid-back first wedding for the flower farm. Nate and Louise wanted low-key and romantic. They were aware that it was a fast wedding date to prepare for and were excited to help. Future weddings would be much more planned. And probably more stressful at times.

Maggie could hardly contain the joy she felt for this venture of making Nate and Louise's dreams come true.

Walking through town, her thoughts meandered to Jake. He had been vague about his plans beyond picking up his car later. When she'd told him her plans, she hoped he'd share his.

It didn't matter; she felt lighter than she had in a long time. It wasn't just her new haircut. She no longer carried the secret of Jake being Oliver's father. And there was Oliver's sudden breakthrough. She felt like it was a new beginning for her. With Jake, she might be cautiously optimistic but wanted to proceed slowly.

She felt a fluttery feeling in her stomach thinking about what Jake said earlier about wanting to get to know her and who she is now. She was just as curious about him.

It moved her that he was genuinely humble and trying hard to make amends to repair his fractured family.

Maggie spotted the hanging baskets of bougainvillea outside the vintage clothes shop on Main Street. She made a beeline for it. There was just enough time to visit before meeting Jake at the Wild Onion Diner.

She found a ton of clothes that appealed to her. A while later, in the dressing room, she realized she'd need help to get her out of there without buying everything she'd tried on. Looking through everything piece by piece, she made some tough decisions. What she was buying went on the hook to the right of the mirror, and what she wasn't on the hook to the left.

Once she was done with her shopping, she stepped outside and met Jake on the sidewalk as she was heading to the truck to stow her purchases. She didn't want to carry all the bags into the diner.

Jake pretended not to recognize her as he walked passed. Then he stopped her. "Excuse me, I'm looking for Maggie Madison. You might know her. About your height, brown hair in a ponytail?" He looked across the street then behind her.

"Very funny, Jake!" Maggie laughed.

"Seriously, you look wonderful. Love the hair!" Jake looked at her with open admiration.

Maggie felt heat flood her face as he held some of the bags for her and she unlocked the truck. Then he waved his arm with a theatrical flourish for her to set her bags inside.

"Stop," Maggie said. Attracting attention in the middle of the town was so not her style.

Jake grinned before becoming serious. "You have to admit the usual rules don't apply to us getting to know each other again."

"I don't know about that. They might," Maggie said.

Jake paused. "Do you want them to, Mags? Proper dating to get to know each other again?"

"Maybe."

Jake smiled. "I can do that."

Maggie's breath caught as he looked into her eyes. Her heart fluttered again.

"I will admit that I'm a bit rusty at sharing my heart," Jake said. Then he slowly leaned forward and kissed her softly.

When they parted, she opened her eyes.

"Maggie," he whispered softly. "Maybe I could be the man you and Oliver need. The man you want in your life."

Maggie held her breath. Maybe she wanted that too. She still wasn't sure…

# *Chapter Twelve*

Maggie Madison rocked his world.

To think he even had the hint of a chance with this beautiful woman sitting across the table from him at the Wild Onion Diner felt absolutely amazing. People kept coming by the table to say hello to her. He saw their genuine affection for her. Just now, she excused herself to talk to a couple who waved to her just as they were about to leave.

It did lead him to wonder how often she actually left the farm. The townspeople seemed to think spotting Maggie in town was a rarity. Apparently she only came into town for business and headed back home again.

She seemed happy with the life she'd made for herself and for Oliver. And that was a blessing. Thinking about what they'd both gone through sometimes seemed unfathomable.

"Sorry about that," Maggie said, shaking him out of his reverie. "That couple I was talking to are the Edwardses. They've been wonderful customers. Every year, they come to the farm to buy flowers for the event they sponsor to raise money for cancer research. Last year, they didn't just buy flowers, they asked us to design and decorate the event! I hope they ask us again. They host a grand gala ball with a different theme each year."

"Do you attend the balls?" Jake asked.

Maggie shook her head no as she took a bite of her jalapeno burger.

"Why not?" he couldn't stop himself from asking.

Maggie finished chewing and wiped her mouth. "I don't dance," she said simply.

Jake was surprised by that. The Maggie he remembered was quite fond of dancing back in the day.

Maggie glanced toward the counter and waved. She seemed pleased to see a man who looked big enough to be a security guard at a concert heading over to their table.

"Jake, this is Brian."

Brian smiled warmly, "Pleased to meet you, Jake."

"Brian is the father of one of the kids Oliver is friends with. He's also one of the high school math teachers," said Maggie.

"And she left out a baritone in the church choir, which I hear you'll soon be directing!" said Brian.

"Whoa, word travels fast. I just spoke to Pastor Luke this afternoon. I haven't even had a chance to tell Maggie yet!" exclaimed Jake.

"Church choir director?" Maggie's face couldn't be more surprised.

"It's just temporary, but yes, I'll be the church choir director. Care to join us, Brian?" Jake asked.

"Mighty nice of you, but I'm heading out. Just devoured a big bowl of chili and cornbread. Enjoy your meal. Be seeing you soon at rehearsal, Jake," Brian said.

"Looking forward to it," Jake said. "I'm going to fix up the place too, so you may not recognize it," teased Jake.

"If you need an extra pair of hands, let me know," said Brian. "In fact," he said as he jotted down his phone number on a piece of paper and handed it to Jake, "don't hesitate to be in touch."

Jake thanked Brian before he walked away.

Leaning toward Maggie, Jake said, "Seems like a good guy."

"One of the best. I like his wife Carol too," Maggie said as she dipped her fry in ketchup.

Jake took a sip of water.

They didn't talk much as they finished the rest of their meal on a happy vibe.

While Jake went to the restroom, Maggie paid the bill, then they stepped out into the beautiful sunshine. "I have some boxes that Gram wants me to deliver to the church," she told him.

"I could have dropped off Gram's things if I'd known. How 'bout I come with you?" Jake suggested.

"Sounds good. We can just grab the boxes from the truck then cut through the park."

"Sounds good."

"Follow me," Maggie said.

Jake smiled. He'd follow her anywhere, but he didn't say so out loud. That would be the complete opposite of taking things slow.

As they neared Old Grace Church, he couldn't get over the fact that he was going to be the new church choir director. This beautiful church stood proudly surrounded by red maple trees. It certainly was a focal point in the town, with its pillars and circular driveway at the entrance. He didn't know much about its history, but he was curious to learn.

He'd be attending church services now. He knew Zoe didn't attend. And he wondered about Maggie and Oliver.

Stepping inside the sanctuary always gave him that hushed tone feeling. Not so much for Maggie, who called out, "Hello! Anyone here?"

A petite older woman hurried out from the back, wiping her hands on a denim apron. "Yes. Hello. I'm Dina."

Maggie held up her box. "Hi! I'm Maggie, and this is Jake."

"Jake Madison, the new choir director?" she asked.

"Yes, ma'am, " he said.

"I'm sorry I wasn't here earlier to meet you. Pastor Luke just headed home if you need to speak to him," Dina said with a worried look on her face.

"No, I'm here helping with these boxes," Jake said.

"We have some items for the children's room." Maggie held up the box she was carrying.

"Oh, yes, I was expecting you. Yvonne called earlier. This way," Dina said.

They had a hard time keeping up with Dina as she practically raced down a long hallway.

Maggie turned toward Jake and grinned.

"In here, if you will." Dina stepped inside the room and pointed toward a table near a window.

Before the boxes made it to the table, Dina called out as she left, "Thank you both. Have a good day!"

"What do you think she's so busy doing?" Maggie asked.

"I haven't a clue," Jake said as he set down his boxes.

"It's such a pretty church," Maggie said wistfully.

"Come with me," Jake said. He led her to the rehearsal room and flipped on the light switch. "My first task is to make this room warm and inviting."

He could see Maggie trying hard not to react, but she couldn't stifle a giggle. "I'd say you have your work cut out for you. You know I'll help."

"And maybe bring over some flowers when it's all done?" Jake asked hopefully.

"You got it," said Maggie.

On their way out, Maggie stopped to take a closer look at some framed calligraphy of Bible quotes and motivational sayings.

"He does such lovely work, doesn't he?" Dina suddenly appeared beside them. "Sorry I rushed off. We were finishing getting boxes of goods to bring to those in need. We're not keeping well to the schedule today, I'm afraid."

"Do you need help?" asked Jake.

"Aren't you nice. But no, thank you. They're all loaded and on their way. As I was saying," Dina pointed to the framed art, "these are so lovely. Especially now that schools don't seem to be teaching cursive anymore. Silly decision, in my opinion."

"I agree," said Maggie. "Do you happen to know if the artist teaches calligraphy classes? I've always been interested in learning how to do it. And, if he's interested, I could also mention him to the brides for their invitations."

Dina pondered for a moment. "I believe he does. I know I've saved his card somewhere. Come with me, dear."

Jake touched Maggie's arm. "I'll just wait for you."

Maggie nodded and hurried off to catch up to Dina.

Sitting on a pew, he admired the stained-glass windows. He closed his eyes for a moment to absorb the peace of his surroundings.

"Thank you again for Gregory's card," he heard Maggie say. "I'm anxious to check out his website."

He stood up just as Maggie spied two buckets of irises of mixed colors. "One of my favorite flowers," she said as she bent over to admire them. "They are the perfect perennials. Drought resistant, hardy, nearly disease- and insect-free. Often, people plant them in front of their homes."

Dina said, "We were so lucky to get these today from a member of the church. A one-time donation. I'm just about to put them into vases.

"Another member of the church, Mrs. Kellogg, used to bring us flowers faithfully, then she sold her house. She moved to Skowhegan to be closer to her daughter and family. We no longer have a steady supply of flowers for services, funerals and celebrations. Sad, really. Flowers bring such joy, don't they?"

Jake watched as Maggie folded her hands in front of her. "I'd be happy to help with the flowers from Maggie's Flower Farm for the church."

The woman furrowed her brows. "Thank you, dear, but we can't afford to buy flowers. Well, maybe some but not every week. I know you do have lovely gardens on the farm."

Jake saw Maggie take a deep breath. "I've been growing some flowers apart from what we sell. Dinner-plate-size dahlias, sunflowers and others. I've wanted them to go to someplace special. I'll give them to you for no charge."

"Oh my dear! Are you sure?" Dina looked hesitant.

Maggie smiled broadly. "I am very sure."

"Could you deliver them when you come to services on Sunday?" Dina asked. "We could keep them as fresh as possible here for our other church needs. Wouldn't want you to have to make special trips. We have a refrigerator."

Jake suppressed a grin when he saw Maggie's eyes widen before answering.

"Yes, um… Sunday services. That would be fine. We could deliver them then," Maggie said.

Jake nodded. He was proud of Maggie. He saw that the offer was snowballing into more than she'd anticipated.

"Can you start this weekend?" Dina asked.

Maggie nodded. Before she could say another word, Dina kissed Maggie's cheek.

"My dear," she said, "I'm so happy He brought you here today to share His beauty with us. Bless you."

"I'm happy to," said Maggie, blushing.

Maggie and Oliver would soon be going to church with Gram and him. That thought made Jake very happy indeed.

*What just happened?*

It felt so right for Maggie to be giving her special flowers to the church in town.

And she'd had the feeling that eventually she'd know who needed them when the time was right. One of the recipients was the animal shelter adoption drive. She delivered buckets of flowers to the fairgrounds. The workers set them near the checkout stand. Also next to the pens of the animals that were up for adoption. People took flowers as well as new furry family members home with them.

Maggie felt blessed to be able to help Gram's Old Grace Church. As she followed Jake toward the front door, a stained-glass window of Jesus in a field of flowers caught her attention. The flowers and the sun shining on them were breathtaking. She squinted. Was Jesus standing near flowers that were the same color as her large dahlias?

Maggie briefly closed her eyes. *Here You are again, God, meeting me where I am. Forgive me for shutting You out a while ago. And thank You for welcoming me back in.*

Jake touched her arm. "It always amazes me to see Him at work. How do you feel about it?"

"It was special, Jake. I knew I'd find where those flowers were meant to go. I thought it would be to sporadic community events. I never dreamed it would be to the entire congregation of Old Grace Church."

"You're not regretting it, are you?"

She heard the concern in Jake's voice. "No, not regretting it for a second. I'm all in. But I am glad I planted so many flowers!" Maggie laughed.

"It's a wonderful gift, Mags. Just think how Gram will feel when you tell her."

His words warmed her heart.

Outside, it was a beautiful summer's day. Kids were running around and playing in the park. She caught a Frisbee as it sailed toward her and sent it back. She laughed joyfully at the thumbs-up from the young girl who caught it.

Would Oliver be out here someday with his friends? She hoped so. Just imagining it made her happy.

And maybe the three of them could have a picnic before Jake left Maine?

Maggie knew Jake would love for Oliver to know the truth of his parentage. And she had to admit, the possibility of revealing the truth didn't seem so far off as she once thought.

Looking for Jake, she saw the Joyful Scoops stand had a small line. Jake had suggested getting shakes. She observed him smiling and chatting with others in line.

Looking around, she spied an empty bench facing the park. Perfect.

She read the plaque on the bench she'd chosen. "This bench is dedicated to my dear wife who visited this park daily with me." She sighed, wondering if they'd lived in one of the homes on the street behind her.

Closing her eyes, she lifted her face to the sun the way her flowers did. Instead of water, though, she'd have a mocha milkshake for sustenance.

Maggie ran her fingers through her new haircut. It felt great to have a few inches chopped off the length.

Surprising herself, she realized she'd only just now thought about the business and checked her phone for messages. There was one text message from Zoe, telling her to have fun.

Today had been fun. It was kind of amazing when she thought about it all.

It surprised her that she and Jake had been comfortable with each other. She had just been herself. She hadn't thrown any defenses up, or at least, not many. They'd talked, joked. He'd flirted. They'd kissed.

She frowned when she wondered what time Jake had told Matt he'd stop by to pick up the car. The thought of it didn't gladden her heart. *Thy will be done, Lord. You know best, not I.*

"Here you go, Mags," Jake said and sat down beside her.

They sipped their milkshakes. Suddenly their enjoyable day was interrupted by a loud bang.

People yelled, "Fire!"

Maggie's pulse raced.

The fire was behind them. Maggie's eyes widened with horror. She felt faint.

A house on fire.

Just as many people ran toward the fire as away from it. People screamed.

She stood up, her milkshake spilling down the front of her.

*Oliver. Where was Oliver? He wasn't here, right?*

Jake's voice called her name. She barely heard it over the roar of the fire trucks and the police car sirens.

Fire!

Maggie broke free from someone trying to grab her arm. Then someone called her name.

She stumbled as she ran toward the fire.

Maggie wove in and out of people until she almost reached the house.

Stopped. Mesmerized.

Large pieces of black charred wood fell to the ground.

A crackling sound.

Her lungs burned when she coughed.

The heat of the fire.

Sweat poured down the side of her face.

She couldn't breathe. Couldn't move.

Glass breaking. Firemen yelling, "Over here! Over here!"

*Oliver. Was he safe? He wasn't here. Right? Good.*

As if from a long dark tunnel, she heard her name.

An arm went around her shoulders to pull her back, away from the fire.

Didn't they understand? Someone could be hurt. She had to help.

Her memory played tricks. She saw a fireman carrying someone out, but then they vanished.

*She wasn't waiting for an ambulance for Oliver.*

*Her life and her belongings weren't in there.*

*Oliver? Not here. Good.*

She turned and saw Jake. What was he doing here?

# *Chapter Thirteen*

Jake's pulse raced as he reached Maggie. He heard her ragged breaths.

What was this? A reaction to the fire? A flashback?

*Keep calm,* he told himself. *Keep calm for Maggie.*

She trembled so much that it scared him.

The color had drained from her face. Her eyes were full of fear.

"Mags?" He needed to break her connection to the fire.

He noted her harsh bark of a cough.

Gently, he stroked her back.

He needed her to focus on *anything* but the fire.

"Maggie, look at me. Please," he begged her.

Relieved, he thought he felt her lean into him a bit.

Firemen started moving people away from the fire.

"Can we turn around, Mags? Or back up a bit?"

She blinked but didn't move.

He wanted to shield her from the view of the fire. To break its hold on her. If he could nudge her body to turn sideways. Palm her face to block the view of the fire.

"Maggie, you're okay. You're okay. You're safe," he kept repeating.

Jake looked at the house, which was fully engulfed now. His stomach lurched. He hoped no one was badly injured.

Just then he heard a fireman on the radio say that no one was hurt. Everyone got out.

"Did you hear that, Mags? Everyone is safe." He sighed with relief, truly grateful that he could tell Maggie that good news.

Her eyes widened. She focused on him. Finally!

*Thank You, God!*

Jake caught her as she started to crumble. He held her as she cried into his shirt.

"Can you make it to the bench over there?" he asked.

She nodded and he kept a tight hold on her as they walked slowly.

"Lean on me, babe. Just lean on me," he said.

Maggie lowered herself gingerly onto the bench.

Jake asked, "Can you take a deep breath for me?"

Maggie shook her head. "Hurts," she croaked out.

"It's all right," Jake reassured her.

She closed her eyes and slumped against him.

Jake spotted Brian in the crowd and waved him over.

Brian broke into a run and knelt down in front of Maggie. A woman followed closely behind. "Maggie, are you okay?" he asked.

"What can we do?" asked the woman.

"Water. Anything wet. Please," Jake said.

"Be right back," she said and took off for the nearest food truck.

"That's my wife, Carol," Brian said to Jake. "Is Maggie having a PTSD episode?"

"I don't know. It could be," answered Jake.

Brian tried to reassure Maggie. "Maggie, it's Brian. Carol is here too. She's getting you something to drink. You're all right."

Maggie didn't open her eyes but nodded. She clutched Jake's shirt. Her fist was digging into his spine, but he didn't care.

Carol returned with a cardboard holder with two large plastic cups of water.

"You need to sip this slowly, both of you," she advised.

"I'm okay," said Jake. His hand shook as he held the cup of water for Maggie.

"Mags, I need you to sip this water. Just a tiny bit."

Maggie opened her eyes. She looked panicked for a moment as she searched for the fire.

He guided her face toward him. "Maggie, look at me. Everything is all right now."

She nodded and slowly loosened her grip on him. Then she reached for the water and held it with both hands.

"Slowly," Brian cautioned.

Maggie took a sip.

Jake was relieved. Her color was coming back. He knew her throat might still be sore, though, from the panic as well as the smoke that had blown their way.

"I—I feel so foolish. Sorry to worry everyone," Maggie said with her eyes downcast.

Carol knelt down in front of her. "Maggie, there's nothing to feel foolish about. Maybe you had a panic attack? A possible PTSD episode? I've been through them. You look better now, though, hon."

Maggie sighed. "I think I'm feeling better now."

"I don't know how to thank you both," Jake said. "I couldn't have left her to get water."

"Glad we were here," Brian said as he handed Jake the other water. "Your voice sounds better than hers, man. But I really think you should drink something too."

"You're right." Jake took the plastic cup and took a slow sip. "Thank you both again," he said.

The men shook hands. Carol squeezed Maggie's shoulder.

"Can you two get home okay?" Brian asked.

Jake looked at Maggie, who nodded.

"Yeah. Pretty sure," said Jake.

"See you soon," Brian said. "We'll stop by the farm and see how you're both doing."

"Sounds good," Jake and Maggie said at the same time. They turned to each other and smiled.

Jake watched Brian and Carol walk away.

He and Maggie continued to slowly sip their water. "How are you?" he asked her.

"I'm better. I just want to go home right now," said Maggie softly.

Jake said, "Home it is."

Standing up, he saw her take one more look at the fire, which was now under control. She turned to Jake, "Oh no, you have to get your car?"

"No problem. I'll call Matt and tell him I'll pick it up another time," he said.

Maggie seemed able to walk, albeit stiffly. He kept his arm around her to steady her.

He had to ask, "Has this happened before?"

"Not for quite a while. It happened a few times in North Carolina. I think the stressors of Oliver the other night, the fire today. I was triggered. Before the fire, I never had attacks."

He felt her body shudder.

"If you hadn't been here… If I'd come to town alone…" Her voice trailed off.

"But I was here, Mags. And Brian and his wife were too. God is watching over you."

She took his hand in hers and gave it a quick squeeze. "Thank you. I need to go home now. I really need to see Oliver," she said.

He opened the truck door and helped her inside.

"All set," she said, and he shut the door.

He wanted to hold her and never let her go.

On the way home, he kept glancing over at her. She seemed deep in thought.

"Jake?"

"Yes?"

"You really should consider using part of the barn for a workshop. That flower stand you built is really wonderful," she said. Then she yawned.

"That's what you've been thinking about?" he asked incredulously.

"I don't want to think about what just happened with the fire. So I was thinking about you and all your hard work," she said.

"Okay." He didn't know what else to say.

"There's just a solitary workbench in there now, but you could kit out the space with tools and stuff. There's plenty of space in one of the side rooms or off to the back. I don't need it all for wedding receptions," she said.

He nodded.

"And Oliver would like it," she added. "More room to work with you on projects."

"That he would," Jake agreed. Father-and-son visions danced in his head.

"Jake, that was a wonderful kiss earlier," she said just before dozing off to sleep.

Jake smiled. After all that happened, she remembered the kiss.

By the next day, Maggie was feeling more herself. She'd been busy most of the morning in the fields, which were always healing for her.

Pocketing her cell phone, she bumped into Jake as he left the office.

"Hey there! How are you feeling?" was the first thing he asked.

"Better," she said. "Though I must say that Hero has been glued to me all day along with Oliver. I had to sit down this morning and explain to him what happened because he could tell that I was distracted, that something had happened."

"Those two know things." Jake chuckled.

"I wanted to tell you that I think your instincts were one-hundred-percent right when you tried to get me to focus on something other than the fire," Maggie said. "I want to learn how to cope if something like that happens again."

"That's a good idea," Jake said.

She studied him a moment before saying, "I hope it won't happen again, but you never know."

"And speaking of Oliver and Hero, here they are now," Maggie said with a smile.

"Please, M-M-Mom, c-c-can we g-go to Gram's house?" Oliver asked.

"You can go anytime, hon," Maggie said.

"B-b-but you need to come with us," Oliver wheedled. "I—I—I have a mission!"

Maggie looked at Jake, who just shrugged his shoulders.

They all arrived at Gram's house to several more boxes of decorations strewn all about for the Sunday school kids. Gram was sitting in the middle of the living room sorting them out. She saw another trip to the church in her future.

"I—I hafta talk to you and M-Mom a-a minute," said Oliver to Jake and Maggie.

It was clear that neither he nor Maggie had any idea what Oliver was up to.

"You kids go ahead. I'll keep sorting," said Gram. "There will be cookies when you get back."

"Do you want to go for a walk with us?" Jake asked.

Oliver nodded. "H-Hero t-too."

Outside, Jake mentioned to Maggie that he had plans drawn for an arched arbor for her upcoming wedding.

"Thank you, Jake!" Maggie was excited and touched he'd

taken the time. Then she turned to Oliver. "Okay, Oliver, what's on your mind?" she asked him.

"D-d-do you know Jesus?" Oliver looked directly at Jake. "Is He y-your friend?"

Maggie saw the surprise on Jake's face. It matched her own.

"Yes, I'd say Jesus is my friend," Jake replied.

"C-c-can you ask him something for m-me?" Oliver said in a serious tone.

Jake looked at Maggie. "He's your and your mom's friend too. You can ask Him anything directly, you know."

Oliver paused to consider this for a moment.

Maggie was glad she had committed to taking him to church every Sunday.

"How about we pray together for what you want?" Jake suggested.

Oliver nodded. He closed his eyes and clasped his hands together. He opened one eye and said, "You—you guys too."

Maggie closed her eyes.

"Jesus, p-p-please heal my m-mom. She's g-g-getting better now like me."

"We ask this in Your name. Amen," concluded Jake.

"Amen," Maggie and Oliver said in unison.

"Good job, Oliver. That was a good prayer," Jake said as he squeezed Oliver's shoulder.

"Thank you, honey. I'm so happy you asked that for me," Maggie said with a hitch in her voice.

"It's o-o-okay, Mom. I knew it was the r-r-right thing to do. Can I go b-b-back and have some cookies?" Oliver said, bouncing on his heels. He was ready to run back to Gram's house.

Maggie nodded and watched her son take off running. His best friend, Hero, close at his side.

"I just realized something," Jake said to her. "I want Oliver to have a faith-based life."

Maggie replied, "So do I, Jake. So do I."

Jake took her hand and squeezed it. Maggie smiled. Quiet contentment spread through her as they walked back to Gram's house.

Inside, Maggie saw Gram still sorting decorations for the kids' room at church. She couldn't wait to tell her the news. "I have something to share with you, Gram."

"Oh?" she answered. Gram was holding something up it the air. "This is the seventh sheep I've found for the manger scene," Gram exclaimed. She perched the very large cutout sheep on a precarious stack of other animals then sat back to give Maggie her full attention.

"Well, you know the special flowers I've been growing for two years?" Maggie began. "The ones I said weren't for business. I said I'd find special people to give them to?"

"Yes?" Gram seemed intrigued. "I told you you'd find who they were meant to go to. You thought it was silly to do it at first. The calling wouldn't let you go, as I recall."

"Exactly. Well, the flowers are going to Old Grace Church for services and various events. Dina said that Mrs. Kellogg has moved and she used to provide the flowers."

Gram sat back in her chair and stared at Maggie. "Yes, she has moved. Well, I'll be. Are you sure?" she asked.

"Of course. I think it's wonderful, but as I told Jake, I'm grateful that I planted so many in that far field." Maggie chuckled. "Imagine! I'm still wrapping my head around it. And Jake will be helping me deliver them when we all go to church services on Sunday."

Gram, who was happily stunned, said, "Praise the Lord! He surely does work in mysterious ways when He answers my prayers!"

Zoe walked in the house and reached for one of Gram's cookies. "These must be pretty good, everyone is in such a good mood."

Gram leaned over to Maggie and whispered, "Now if I could just get her to church."

Maggie smiled but didn't say anything.

Jake turned to Oliver. "I have a surprise for you." Jake left and came back with three guitars.

"I know you like music. Do you want to learn to play the guitar?" he asked Oliver.

Oliver's head bobbed up and down.

Maggie pointed to one and said, "That was your first guitar, wasn't it?" Then she pointed to a second guitar, an early Martin. "I bet that one is worth beaucoup bucks!"

Zoe piped up, "Not to mention, these are a country rock star's early guitars!"

"Enough with the country rock star thing," said Jake.

Oliver was clearly in awe as he absentmindedly rubbed Hero's head.

"I remember that you write songs," said Jake.

Oliver nodded his head.

"Would you like to learn to play the guitar and maybe sing your songs?" asked Jake.

Maggie watched Oliver. She didn't think his eyes could grow any wider.

"Yes. With all m-m-my heart," Oliver said.

Both Gram and Zoe were getting misty-eyed.

Maggie was learning more about her son. He loved dogs and now guitars.

"Well, Oliver," said Jake, "you can try them all out tomorrow once I get them tuned up. Then you can let me know which guitar is your favorite and it's yours. And I'll teach you to play, how's that? With your mom's approval, of course."

Oliver looked at Maggie, a touch of pink in his cheeks and still wide-eyed. How could she say no? She smiled weakly and gave a quick nod. Oliver grinned and ran over to Jake. He hugged him so tight they almost both fell over.

Jake looked at everyone. "I think that's a yes."

Everyone laughed except Maggie.

It had been a long day, and Oliver was already asleep.

He'd been excited all evening about the prospect of learning to play the guitar. Maggie thought spending time with Jake might have something to do with it.

She made herself a cup of chamomile tea and inhaled the steam. Maggie wondered if Oliver learning to play the guitar was a good idea. He sometimes became frustrated easily when learning something new. This would be connected to his writing, which he enjoyed. But singing?

She had to admit that she'd been stunned when Jake asked Oliver if he wanted to learn to play. It would have been better if Jake had asked her first, privately. She might have asked Jake and Oliver questions about expectations, even talked it over with Oliver's counselor.

Maggie pinched the bridge of her nose. Paul had always thought Jake learning to play the guitar was partly responsible for Jake's leaving. It certainly had given him the opportunity to play in the band. Paul wouldn't listen to No Caution under any circumstances. And she felt pretty sure that Paul wouldn't have approved of Oliver learning to play.

So much had changed, though. When Maggie listened to the band's music after Paul's death, she enjoyed most of it. Especially the melancholy tone on some of the songs. And Jake wasn't playing with the band now. His musical talents had taken a different route. Music ministry to worship and praise God.

Giving Oliver another way to communicate could be a blessing. She realized that she needed to trust Jake on this.

Finally feeling like she could relax enough to go to sleep, she took her cup to the kitchen before making her way to bed.

Upstairs, Maggie heard music outside her second-story bedroom window. Lately, she had heard the sounds of Jake singing and playing guitar drifting faintly from Gram's porch. Tonight it sounded much closer.

Pushing aside the curtain, she looked out. What was Jake doing sitting out there on a rock, strumming his guitar in her front yard?

Maggie opened the window wide and called out, "Whatcha doin'?"

"Singing to the moon, Mags. Singing you to sleep," he said.

Maggie felt waves of tension just wash away. She listened to the music for a few minutes before deciding to join Jake outside.

"I'd say that you'll wake the neighbors but I looked in on Oliver and he's fast asleep. And we don't have any other close neighbors except Zoe and Gram," said Maggie.

"And both of them are used to me playing by now." Jake laughed and set his guitar down beside him.

"Seriously, singing me to sleep?" Maggie asked.

"You've been through a lot lately, Mags. I just thought it might help. Granted I don't know any lullabies," he quipped.

"Such a romantic gesture, Jake Madison," Maggie said.

Moments passed as they simply gazed into each other's eyes in the moonlight.

Maggie swayed a bit and suddenly yawned.

"Go to bed, Mags. I'll play a couple more songs and head home. Sweet dreams," Jake said.

Maggie nodded. The past and the present felt like they were colliding. Questions and feelings swirled. "Thank you," she said softly and headed inside.

# *Chapter Fourteen*

The next morning, he asked himself just what he was doing.

What felt right.

His faith, his music, his family that now included a son. A son who he'd soon be teaching how to play the guitar.

Now he was the church's choir director. *Temporarily.*

And he had sat outside Maggie's house singing to her in hopes it would help her sleep.

Jake realized how much he wanted to be there for her, Oliver, and the rest of his family.

He sat on a park bench after Gram dropped him off in town, waiting for Matt to get back from lunch so he could finally pick up his car. Behind him, he saw the remains of the house that burned. He imagined it would be bulldozed and a new house would be built in its place.

Despite everything that had happened yesterday, Jake felt that things had progressed between him and Maggie.

He thought it might be time to talk to Pastor Joe in Kansas, beyond sending scenic postcards and a few hasty texts.

He checked his phone and saw it was fully charged. He knew Maine was an hour ahead of Manhattan, Kansas.

Joe answered quickly. "Jake, I can't believe it! How are you, my friend?"

"Am I calling at a good time?" Jake asked.

"Perfect timing," the pastor said.

It felt as if they were in the same room together and no time had passed at all.

"You're working as a choir director? That's wonderful!" Pastor Joe exclaimed.

"It's temporary, but I'm thinking about applying for it for full-time," Jake said.

"Really?" his friend asked.

"I'm considering it. For so many reasons," Jake said.

"I'm not surprised you're thinking about staying in Maine. Family is family," said Pastor Joe.

The two men found themselves discussing different ways to get Jake's belongings to Maine if he decided to pursue the job full-time.

"You must be missing that Harley of yours!" Pastor Joe kidded him.

Jake still couldn't talk about Oliver being his son without choking up. It was awkward, and people he knew were nearby.

"I hope to meet Maggie as well as the rest of your family," said Pastor Joe.

"You have a standing invitation to come to Maine anytime, my friend."

At the end of their conversation, the pastor said, "Let me know when the wedding will be, and I'll come and officiate."

"What?" Jake exclaimed.

The pastor broke out laughing. "Ah, Jake. I have a feeling we'll talk again soon. Be well, my friend."

As Jake ended the call, he heard Pastor Joe still laughing on the other end.

When Jake turned into the drive at the farm, it felt good to have his own vehicle again. Jake glanced at the clock. Five thirty. It had been a long day, and Jake already felt ready for bed.

As he pulled up to the front of the house, nearly everyone was sitting on Gram's porch drinking lemonade.

Zoe teased, "So that's the clunker that broke down?"

"Hey, it made it here all the way from Kansas. Just a few miles short of the farm," said Jake.

Oliver and Hero appeared from around the back.

Hero stared at the car and gave Jake a withering look.

Oliver was concerned. "Hero, what's the matter?"

Hero kept backing farther and farther away.

Jake was dumbfounded. "Hero, come here, boy. Come here." He slapped his hands on his thighs.

Hero stopped, took another long look at the car, turned and ran straight for the woods.

Jake rubbed his forehead as he watched Hero disappear.

Oliver was upset and started to cry. Maggie tried to calm him. "Hero will be back, Oliver. He will," she said as she looked at Jake.

Bewildered, Jake knelt down on one knee. "Let's find him together, okay?" Jake asked Oliver.

Oliver stopped crying and said, "Okay."

Jake took hold of Oliver's hand. Everyone started walking toward the woods, calling out Hero's name.

"I don't know what to think. That was Hero's reaction to the car?" Jake shook his head.

Gram said, "Jake, I don't think that dog wants to leave."

Jake knew *that* feeling.

Soon it was getting dark out. They all headed back into the house. Oliver was still very agitated and worried.

Suddenly, Jake had an idea on how to get Hero back.

"Gram, I think I need to move the car out by the road. Get it out of sight tonight. I don't think that dog will come back until I relocate the car." Jake and Oliver moved the car and walked back.

Sure enough, half an hour later, Hero finally appeared. He sniffed around near where the car had been parked. Then followed Gram inside to be fed. But not before Oliver threw his arms around Hero.

Relieved that Hero came back, both Maggie and Oliver headed home.

"See you for our first guitar lesson." Jake's heart melted at Oliver's thumbs-up in reply. He loved the idea that he would be teaching Oliver to play the guitar. It would give them a chance to bond. And he hoped Oliver might even learn to love music.

Joining Zoe on the porch, he said, "Seriously, it looks like I have to get another vehicle. I'm fond of Gram's truck. Maybe I should buy a pickup."

"Are you sure? It's a long drive to Kansas. Not to mention you'll have to get a truck cap to keep your stuff out of the weather, dry and safe."

Gram joined them on the porch.

"I'm not so sure I'm going back to Kansas," stated Jake.

"Ever?" asked Zoe incredulously.

"Maybe to visit," Jake said.

"Does Maggie know about this?" Gram asked, eyes wide.

"No, I haven't decided for sure." He ran his fingers through his hair.

"All your stuff is there," said Zoe. "How will you get it here?"

"I just spoke with Pastor Joe in Kansas. It can be worked out," said Jake just as his phone rang. "Excuse me, I have to take this." He went inside with Hero following closely behind him.

"Hi Matt, this is Jake. I'm calling about two things."

"Hit me," Matt said.

"First, I'm bringing the car back. It's running fine. But I need to sell it and I need to park somewhere other than here before it is sold," said Jake.

"Ah, okay, strange but can do," said Matt.

"Second, do you really think we can have the carriage ready in time for the wedding?" Jake asked.

"Yes. You know if it's mechanical, I'm your guy. We can do it," Matt said.

"I have some more ideas I'd like to run by you when you have time," Jake said hopefully.

"Oh, I'll make the time for them," Matt said.

Jake smiled as he hung up and headed out to rejoin Gram and Zoe.

He stopped when he overheard the conversation on the porch as he got closer.

"Wow, Gram, I did not see that coming!" declared Zoe.

"Didn't you?" asked Gram.

"You're right. I guess I kind of did see it. He does seem happy being back in Maine with all of us."

Opening the screen door, Jake and Hero joined them once more on the porch.

Jake had a grin that he just couldn't hide.

"Care to share, boy?" asked Gram.

"Not just yet, I have a plan that I hope comes together," Jake said. Whistling, he sat down on the steps with Hero at his side.

Maggie was glad to be home with Oliver. It had been a long day. And the phone call with his therapist was still ahead.

When the phone rang, Maggie thought the therapist was calling early but it was Zoe.

"Just calling to remind you that Nate and Louise are coming by the office in the morning," Zoe said.

"Great, I'll have the planner ready," Maggie replied.

"And Molly wants to take some photos," Zoe said and added, "I am not sure what she has in mind."

"Guess we'll find out tomorrow," Maggie said. "Thank you for the reminders."

"And, um…have you, has Jake talked about his plans?" Zoe asked tentatively.

Maggie tensed. Zoe wasn't usually so indirect. Clearly, something was on her mind.

"Zoe, what are you talking about? Jake's plans?" she asked.

"Never mind," said Zoe quickly.

"Zoooeee?" Maggie dragged out her name. "What do you know?"

"Nothing really. I'm not sure of anything yet. And neither is he," said Zoe mysteriously.

Maggie hesitated but didn't push. "If there's something I should know, you'll tell me, right?"

"Yes. Or he will," said Zoe. "I really don't know anything definitive."

"Okay. But you know a heads-up would be appreciated," Maggie stressed.

"Understood. See you in the morning," Zoe said and hung up.

*Too mysterious*, thought Maggie.

Oliver distracted her from thinking about the conversation.

"M-Mom, do you think Hero c-can sleep over? S-stay here more often?" asked Oliver.

"I don't know. Maybe. Gram, Zoe and Jake might miss him at night though," suggested Maggie.

"Oh, m-maybe. But Gram says he s-snores. And it's l-loud!" Oliver said.

Maggie chuckled. "Well, that might keep us awake."

"Th-that would be all right, wouldn't it?" asked Oliver.

Maggie smiled. "I suppose so."

"I l-like J-Jake. I don't c-call him Uncle J-Jake often. Do you think he m-minds?" Oliver asked.

Maggie's stomach tightened. Maggie assured him, "I don't think he minds at all."

"Th-that's good. I—I'm going to study guitar chords on-l-line, okay?" Oliver asked.

"Fine with me. I have an important phone call in a little bit," said Maggie.

She listened for Oliver's footsteps and heard his door close.

So many questions swirled in her head.

She wondered if Jake would buy another car to return to Kansas. Obviously, Hero wasn't keen on getting in the one Jake brought home. Did Hero simply not want to return to Kansas?

She was still stunned at the dog's reaction. More importantly though was Oliver's reaction when Hero ran off.

As wonderful as Hero was for Oliver, Maggie was beginning to worry. Oliver was deeply attached to Hero. In many ways, Hero had been an integral part of Oliver's healing.

She should speak to Jake about preparing Oliver for when he and Hero returned to Kansas.

Maggie didn't want her son to be devastated. She didn't want it to be a backwards step in his healing.

She knew she had to prepare herself for the inevitable as well.

Right now though, she wanted to focus on the positive. She was thankful Oliver was up in his room studying guitar chords.

She knew he was doing well. She held on to that to keep herself calm as she settled on the couch in the living room. Finally her phone rang.

"Hello, Maggie! You must be happy about Oliver's progress," said his therapist.

Maggie sat back. "Yes, I am. We all are."

"Good! I'll come straight to the point. As you know we had our second drawing session recently," the therapist said.

"I know you had some concerns about the first one with everyone being so far apart," said Maggie.

"I did, and now I have a question. Do you know someone in Oliver's life who wears a cowboy hat and may have a dog? The father you mentioned, perhaps?" she asked Maggie.

"Yes, that's most likely Jake and Hero. Oliver doesn't know yet that Jake is his father."

"Let me email a photo of his art rather than describe it to

you," she suggested. "I'd say there is already quite a bond forming."

Maggie waited anxiously for the email to come through. What she saw next warmed her heart.

In the center of the picture was Oliver standing next to Maggie. Gram and Zoe stood on the left. Jake with Hero on the right A clear row, no one separated or standing apart from Oliver. In fact, he was in the center and not facing the wall.

"That's wonderful," Maggie exclaimed

She breathed a sigh of relief. She'd been on edge about this phone call all day. And then the car episode with Jake and Hero.

"We've really seen some wonderful improvement, haven't we? I feel so hopeful," said Maggie.

"Yes, so do I. And more good news, I'm pleased to tell you that he is also improving his socialization skills. He's mentioned several names of friends he's made at camp."

"It's true," said Maggie. "I was so pleased that in town, some young people waved and called out his name."

"We want to continue to build on developing his strengths and coping strategies," the therapist said.

Maggie immediately thought about her earlier concerns relating to Jake and Hero's departure for Kansas.

Oliver's therapist continued, "I'm very happy I could give you this good news. Hope you have a good rest of your evening."

"You as well. You made my night!" said Maggie. She hung up the phone, leaned back, closed her eyes and prayed. *Thank You, God!*

The good news made Maggie's heart feel lighter. For all of her list-making of pros and cons and the nights she spent lying awake, she knew now it had been a good idea for Oliver to attend Camp Pine Tree.

Overall, Oliver was healing, Maggie could see it and feel it. She just had to make sure it kept happening.

# *Chapter Fifteen*

Maggie still had the planner in her hand throughout the next morning when meeting with Nate and Louise, the bride- and groom-to-be. They were a joy to work with. They handed her the seating chart for the small wedding. Louise offered to help prepare the small vases of flowers for the tables when it was time. And they had already helped with assembling the gift bags. Maggie was thankful they were willing to be so hands-on. And Louise was thrilled there would be dahlias, small snowberries and gladioli available. They were her favorite flowers.

After Nate and Louise left, Maggie heard hammering and walked out to where Jake and Oliver were working on a wedding arbor. Oliver handed him tools while Hero stood there watching them both intently.

She marveled that somehow Jake found the time to work on projects for the wedding venue. He had projects he was working on for Gram. Guitar lessons to plan. He was the new choir director. And he seemed to take everything in stride, whistling as he worked.

"M-Mom!" Oliver called out. Jake waved from the ladder. Her insides did funny things when she saw the three of them working together.

"It's looking beautiful," she said as she approached.

"Molly is looking for you, Mags. She asked me if Nate and Louise were still here," said Jake.

"No, they already left," Maggie said. "But she can phone them with any questions."

"No, I can't," said Molly, walking up to her from the direction of the office.

Maggie frowned. "They were heading into town, I think."

Molly shifted her camera gear. "You know what, I think you and Jake will do nicely."

"Will do for what?" Jake asked.

"I see you have several photo ops set up around the grounds. I just wanted to get some test shots with the couple," Molly said. "We can start here." Molly pointed out places to stand. "Groom here. And bride here."

Maggie looked at Jake. He looked as uncomfortable as she felt.

"C-c-can I c-carry the rings for you both?" asked Oliver.

"Honey, this is just pretend," said Maggie.

"I—I know." Oliver sighed.

Molly positioned them. Then she started snapping photos.

Next she wanted them standing closely together in front of one of the trellises. "Put your arm around her, Jake."

Maggie could sense his nervousness. Having Jake this up close and personal wasn't easy. Jake gave her shoulder a squeeze, which pulled her closer against him for a moment.

"Oliver, why don't you stand in front with Hero, just for fun."

Oliver couldn't move fast enough. He clearly wanted to be involved in the action, not on the sidelines. Hero plopped down on Jake's boots.

"Oof, take it easy," Jake said as he pulled his feet out from underneath his dog.

That helped ease some of the tension Maggie felt. She set her hands on Oliver's shoulders, and he leaned back onto her.

"Perfect, perfect," Molly said.

Then they headed into the barn where tables and chairs would be set up for the wedding.

"There will be lights in here. Fairy lights and some rafter lights as well," said Maggie.

"Understood," said Molly. "I'm quite excited about this new venture. I gave Louise and Nate the name of a good videographer, and they hired her. They'll have wonderful memories of their special day."

Maggie nodded. She stood there holding hands with Jake. She felt him looking intently at her.

*Please don't let me blush.*

"Perfect," said Molly. "I truly appreciate it, you two."

"Our pleasure," said Jake.

Maggie wasn't so sure about that.

She looked at Jake, and he winked. Clearly he was trying to make light of the situation.

*Don't be so serious,* Maggie scolded herself.

"Back to work, Oliver," Jake said.

Maggie watched as Jake, Oliver and Hero headed back out into the sunshine.

"Do you want any of the photos I shot today?" Molly asked Maggie.

*More than anything*, thought Maggie, but she simply said, "That would be nice. Thank you."

"You got it. Okay, I'm off. I'll visit Zoe before I head out," said Molly.

Maggie sat down on the same spot in the barn where she told Jake that Oliver was his son. She turned when she heard footsteps. Oliver and Hero had returned.

"M-Mom, Jake sent us b-back to check on you," Oliver said as he sat down beside her.

"I don't know why, honey," Maggie said brightly. "I'm fine."

Hero poked her knee.

Maggie laughed. Then said, "Thank you both for checking on me." Maggie hugged Oliver and patted Hero.

"I'm going for my m-m-music lesson soon. And J-J-Jake

gave me this to g-g-give you." Oliver pulled out one of Gram's blueberry bars.

Maggie kissed her son on the cheek, then waved to him as boy and dog walked away.

As she savored the sweet treat, Maggie recalled her dream last night. Standing in a field, Paul and Oliver wore catcher's mitts as they played catch with a baseball. Paul suddenly pointed to Jake, and they waved to each other. Oliver ran toward Jake. Paul turned and waved at her next just before she woke up. Was it a sign to tell Oliver about his father sooner rather than later?

But when?

Maggie worked in the flower fields afterward to help calm her nerves. She thought about Nate and Louise's wedding next month and hoped all went well. She was thrilled to be a part of couples starting their lives together. The flowers would be like beautiful songs of celebration.

Hours went by as she pruned and gathered flowers for the church. Then she headed back into the barn. Earlier she'd glimpsed several very large terra-cotta pots. She wheeled them out one at a time on a dolly. They'd clean up beautifully and look great with flowers in them. Maybe they'd lend an Italian villa feel to the wedding venue.

Sitting down on a white wrought-iron bench in the sun, she scrubbed the dirt off the pots with a brush and mild soap. Then she'd soak them in a fifty-fifty white vinegar and water mixture to dissolve any mineral deposits and let them air dry to prevent mold.

Zoe joined her. "Need a hand?" she asked as she pulled a pair of gloves from her back pocket.

"Always," Maggie answered and scooched over on the bench.

Zoe pulled on her gloves. "Boy, we're lucky Hurricane Duncan is headed out to sea. It did a number south of us."

Maggie shivered. "Yes, it's been a destructive monster!"

"I saw you and Jake posing as a happy couple," Zoe said as she maneuvered a pot closer to her.

Maggie remained silent.

"You two do make a good couple," Zoe said, not looking at Maggie.

Maggie shook her head. Words failed her.

"You guys can always do the long-distance thing, you know," suggested Zoe.

"Really? I don't think so," Maggie said. "Maine to Kansas?"

"Never say never," Zoe said.

"I have my hands full with the business and Oliver. I'm not interested in a relationship that would make life even more difficult for me."

"Life has a way of working itself out, you know?" said Zoe. "And Oliver is doing so much better these days."

"You sound like Gram," Maggie chuckled.

"I know. I'm very wise," Zoe said.

Maggie chuckled as her cell phone buzzed with a text message. It was Jake saying she might want to stop by during his first music lesson with Oliver.

*That's curious.*

Maggie was happy the two of them shared a love of music. *Like father like son.*

Maggie had looked up what Jake's guitars had cost, but it hadn't fazed him. And she was deeply touched when Jake said, "What's mine is his."

Jake told her he'd keep the vintage guitars for lessons and for Oliver to practice on at home. He told her he planned to buy an acoustic guitar with a pickup, strap, case and picks for Oliver. He could take that one to school or wherever he wanted to go with it.

Maggie texted Jake to ask where they were.

Jake texted back, We're out back of the barn. Bring something to sit on. What I'm witnessing is pretty amazing.

Maggie had no idea what he was talking about but was curious to find out.

At the house, she grabbed a plaid throw and headed to the back of the barn. On the way, she spotted some wild purple bergamot flowers. The bees were as happy as she was to see them. Bergamot was a beneficial plant for insects as well as hummingbirds and butterflies.

Nearing the music lesson, she saw Hero right beside Oliver and smiled.

As she got closer, she overheard Jake. "Music is everywhere. It's birdsong. It's Gram's chimes tinkling in the wind."

"It's in the b-background of c-computer games," Oliver said.

Jake nodded. "Totally. I have some music software programs. One is about the instruments and what they can do. And we can work with the songs you write too, if you want to," he added.

Maggie heard Oliver's enthusiastic response. Jake didn't know what he was getting himself into. Oliver was obsessed with computer games.

She called out to them as she approached. "Mind if I sit and listen for a bit?"

Hero got up and met her, hoping to be petted. She didn't disappoint him.

Oliver grinned and waved her over.

Jake said with a wink, "If it's all right with my guy here, it's okay with me."

Maggie smiled as she spread out the blanket she brought and sat a little ways from them.

Jake had Oliver choose a song from their sheet music. The two started strumming to warm up.

"Recognize it?" Jake asked her.

"I do," Maggie said. It was a popular tune from the seventies that Jake used to sing to Maggie when they were younger.

Jake nodded. "It's only got four chords. G, C, D and E."

Oliver worked on his finger changes and maintaining rhythm. He couldn't seem to get it right and stopped in frustration.

Hero nudged his arm. Oliver moved away, and Hero nudged again.

"Oh, all right!" Oliver said angrily and tried again. The third time was a charm.

Jake caught Maggie's attention. He looked her in the eye and nodded toward Oliver.

Oliver began singing.

*Word for word. Without stuttering.*

*How is this even possible?*

Maggie tried to remember if she'd ever heard him sing. She hadn't. Did he sing when she wasn't listening?

There was no hiss of soft consonants. No halting.

All the words had no trace of a stutter.

Maggie stared at Jake, bewildered. Oliver kept singing strong and true. Both of their eyes brimmed with unshed tears, and they quickly blinked and wiped them away.

"Oliver," Jake said, "that's pretty amazing."

Oliver beamed.

"Honey—" Maggie's voice broke "—that was beautiful. I loved it. Do you know that you don't stutter when you sing?"

Oliver nodded, grinning. "I—I found my v-v-voice. In the m-m-music." He looked at Jake and asked, "Right, Jake?"

"Right! I think that's good for today, don't you?" Jake asked him.

Oliver nodded. "I'll g-go play with Hero."

"Sure, honey," Maggie said, giving him a side hug before he left.

"Why didn't you tell me?" asked Maggie.

Jake laughed. "I thought you'd want to experience it firsthand. And you know, I couldn't deprive myself of your beautiful smile."

Maggie blushed. "It was so amazing. I had no idea."

"It has to do with the way we alter our vocal chords to sing. And the way that we shape our mouths and tongues differently than speaking. It's fascinating."

Maggie thought for a moment. "And no one is waiting for a response with singing as in speaking. No pressure."

Jake nodded. "Maggie, I can't tell you how much I'm going to love sharing music with Oliver. Teaching him to play guitar. Hearing his voice clear and strong. Today he really felt the music. Thank you."

"Thank me? Thank *you.* You're the one working with him," said Maggie. Suddenly overcome with emotion, she couldn't say anything more.

Jake reached out and took Maggie's hand. "I love being here for you and Oliver," Jake said. "It means a lot that you trust me to teach Oliver. To share my love of music with him."

Something inside her shifted. She did trust Jake. Not just with Oliver but maybe with her heart as well.

After the lesson, Oliver ran ahead back to the house with Hero.

Maggie and Jake chatted as the colors of evening were deepening quickly. Soon they'd fade into the evening shadows.

Jake loved seeing Maggie smile as she shared her day with him. Her work in the field and the terra-cotta pots she'd found. She glowed with the happiness of having a successful day.

As they neared her house, Maggie asked him if he wanted to sit on the porch for a while. She offered him some lemonade that she'd made yesterday.

Jake couldn't resist. They settled in on the long bench with comfy cushions.

"You haven't mentioned much about the choir director job."

Jake smiled. It surprised him just how much he was enjoying it.

"The choir is coming along well. They feel more cohesive

now. Having a place to gather before and after practice is wonderful," Jake said.

"And you like working as a choir director?" Maggie asked before taking a long sip of lemonade.

"I do. They are a wonderful group of people. We're all bonding, especially in musical and spiritual goals," Jake said.

Maggie smiled. "That doesn't surprise me. It sounds like you're making a real impact on their lives."

"I've shared some of my life experiences with them. Pastor Luke will also be involved in guiding and supporting the choir." Jake rubbed his neck. "You know, it surprised me they said they hadn't ever discussed the deeper meaning behind the songs before. They just more or less memorized them to sing at services."

"Sounds like you're the right person at the right time to bring this choir together," Maggie said warmly.

Jake turned to look at her. "Mags, I have something to ask you regarding the choir," Jake said.

Maggie laughed. "Oh, please don't ask me to sing! You'll totally regret it."

Jake smiled and shook his head. "No, I really want to ask what you think about asking Oliver if he'd like to sing in the choir."

Maggie blinked several times.

"Really? I know he's familiar with songs during services, but, he doesn't sing along," Maggie said cautiously.

"You heard him today. He doesn't stutter when he sings. How wonderful is that? I asked Pastor Luke if there was an age requirement for the choir, and there isn't one."

Jake couldn't gauge how Maggie was really feeling about his request.

"I think if he wants to, it's all right with me. I worry about his frustration level, though, if he feels he isn't getting things right. If it all makes him nervous, he'll stutter and be uncomfortable. And how will the others react to him being in the choir? They're all adults," Maggie said.

Trying to address her concerns, he suggested, "I'll be there to help him. Maybe Hero could be there?"

"You want Hero in the choir as well?" Maggie laughed.

"Well, not exactly," Jake said. "Though the times I've brought him with me, the members loved him being there."

Maggie nodded.

Jake continued, "As to how they'll feel, I don't know. If it makes you feel better, I can ask the choir beforehand. My impression of them as a whole is they are warm and caring. And Oliver may not want to even do it. We won't know unless we ask."

"I guess you're right," Maggie said.

"Okay?" Jake asked.

"I think so," said Maggie quietly.

Jake heard Oliver and Hero running near the house.

Maggie called out Oliver's name, and they both arrived, out of breath, at the foot of the porch stairs.

"Jake has something to ask you, honey," said Maggie.

Oliver went up and sat on the top stair. Hero flopped down on the porch beside him, clearly ready to rest a bit.

Jake cleared his throat first. "Oliver, you seem to really enjoy music and singing. You know I'm working with the church as the choir director. What would you think about joining the choir?" Jake asked.

Jake noticed that Oliver instinctively reached out to touch Hero. Then Oliver looked at Maggie, who smiled at him.

"It's totally up to you, sweetheart," she said.

"I—I don't know," he said as he fidgeted. One hand on Hero, he rubbed the leg of his jeans with the other hand.

"That's perfectly fine. You can think about it," said Maggie softly.

"Take all the time you want," said Jake.

Maggie asked Oliver if he wanted some lemonade and Jake if he wanted a refill. Both answered in the affirmative.

When she returned with glasses and a dog treat for Hero, Oliver spoke up.

"Are there any other k-k-kids in the ch-choir?" he asked tentatively.

Jake shook his head. "No, but that's a good idea. Maybe some kids might want to join in the future."

"M-m-maybe if they see me s-sing, they'll w-w-want to join?" Oliver wondered out loud.

"Maybe," said Jake.

Oliver lowered his head. "What if I—I st-st-stutter?" he asked.

"You can participate as much or as little as you are comfortable with. So far, when I've heard you sing, you haven't stuttered," Jake said.

"I d-don't when I sing," Oliver said emphatically. "I—I think I'd like to t-t-try!" Oliver declared. "Th-thank you f-f-for asking me!"

"I think it will be fun, Oliver. We'll bring Hero too," Jake said.

"Yessss!" Oliver fist pumped the air.

Jake could see the happiness and hope on Maggie's face.

"C-can I—I go watch television, M-Mom?" Oliver said as he got to his feet. Hero staggered to his feet as well. They'd clearly worn each other out.

"Sure, honey. I'm happy you're going to give choir a try." Maggie smiled.

"That's amazing," Maggie said once Oliver and Hero were inside.

"I feel the same way," said Jake. "I promise to make sure he doesn't overdo it with the choir."

"I know he'll be fine with you, Jake," said Maggie confidently.

"Are you still certain you don't want to join too?" Jake teased.

Maggie didn't answer except to yawn.

He slid closer and put his arm around her. She laid her head on his shoulder.

"Oliver has come so far this summer," she said.

They sat there together, enjoying each other's company.

Jake talked a bit more about teaching Oliver to play the guitar, which led him to want to share his feelings about Maggie. His heart thundered in his chest.

She was quiet. He felt emboldened as he drew in a deep breath and then said, "Maggie, there hasn't been another woman for me. I love you."

No response. He'd gone too far. It was too soon.

Jake looked down at her head still on his shoulder. She was asleep.

He wanted so badly to laugh but didn't. He laid his head on hers and inhaled the flowery scent of her shampoo, content to let her sleep until both their phones rang.

Maggie woke up with a jump. Jake answered his phone first.

"Yes, we're both here, Zoe. Wait a sec, let me put you on speaker."

Oliver's footsteps thundered down the stairs from inside the house.

The door to the porch flew open. "M-Mom, a st-st-storm is c-c-coming!"

# Chapter Sixteen

Maggie bolted upright. The last she heard was that Hurricane Duncan was headed out to sea.

Jake stood up, holding his phone in front of him so they could all hear Zoe. "The remnants of Hurricane Duncan turned inland. Now it's due to hit Maine as strong lines of storms. Winds, rain, flash flooding, thunderstorms."

Maggie hugged Oliver. She tried to take it all in. There was so much to do. Protect the flowers as best they could. Also, the structures for the wedding venue…

"We'll see you both soon," Jake said as he ended the call.

Jake looked as stunned as she felt.

"S-s-saw it on the computer," Oliver said. Maggie hugged him closer.

"Good job for letting us know," Jake said.

Maggie slipped her arm away from Oliver's back and stood up. "We have to see the news. Then I need to make a list of what must be done on the farm."

Jake touched her arm. "You're not alone, Mags. I'm here to help. I can move some of the structures I've been working on inside the barn."

Maggie nodded.

The news on TV was even more alarming. Their window of time wasn't days. It was closer to hours.

Zoe and Gram came bursting in the door.

"What do you need, Maggie? I've closed the storm shutters on my house," Gram said. "I can do the ones here."

"Yes, please," Maggie said with a shudder. Reality was hitting her. She needed to round up all the stakes and cages and ringed fabric sheeting to attach to the rebar stakes. Fortunately, she had these things stowed in the barn in case of emergency.

"It's going to be a long night," said Jake as he headed out the door to the barn. Hero stayed close behind.

Maggie dug out all the rain gear she could find in the closet.

Gram waited on the porch, looking up at the sky. Maggie could tell she was praying.

Outside, Maggie noticed the ominous low-level clouds moving their way.

"I can already feel the wind picking up," Gram said.

Hero shadowed Oliver, who ran ahead toward the barn.

Maggie gripped the front of her slicker. She really hoped they could get everything done before the storm hit.

"Just tell us what you need us to do," said Gram as she linked arms with Maggie.

Reaching the barn, Maggie's stomach flipped as she looked at the vast amount of necessary materials Jake had amassed.

Jake looked calmer than he felt, Maggie was sure of it, and she admired him for that.

"I was thinking Oliver and I could take down the willow trellis and some of the smaller wooden structures we've been working on and bring them in here," said Jake.

Maggie nodded. Anything they could save would be a blessing.

"I need to get the sheeting over the flowers ASAP," said Maggie. She jumped as she heard a loud crash.

Jake hurried outside and reported back. "A branch of a tree broke off. The wind is definitely picking up."

Maggie, Zoe and Gram dragged out sheeting to cover the rows of flowers. They needed to tie the sheeting to the rebar stakes that were already in place. The one time they'd done this before was for a much smaller storm. Thankfully they started out working like a well-oiled machine on the rows.

Jake's voice carried on the wind. "Hold that end as steady as you can," he called out to Oliver.

Rain squalls now accompanied the stronger winds that had finally hit. Maggie had no idea how much time had passed. She stood up to straighten out her aching back.

"Gram, do you want to rest before the next row?" Maggie asked.

"I'm all right, but have you two seen Jake and Oliver?" Gram asked Zoe and Maggie with a worried expression.

Maggie looked around.

"There," Zoe shouted and pointed at Jake hammering boards over the windows on the greenhouses while Oliver handed him nails. Hero circled the greenhouses as if inspecting them.

Maggie hoped the line of trees she'd planted would help to act as a buffer.

"Back to work, girls," said Gram with a smile.

Maggie and Zoe agreed as they opened another package of sheeting and began unrolling it.

The rain squalls felt more like driving rain now. And the wind whipped.

"Maggie, I heard thunder in the distance. We can't stay out here in thunder and lightning," Jake said as he approached her with rain pelting his face. "We'll have to head in soon."

She didn't want to stop what she was doing but knew she had to. Maggie nodded and said, "All hands on deck for the sheeting then."

"Tie it down this way, Oliver," Jake instructed. "No storm is going to rip that off. At least I hope not," he added.

The storm was getting closer, and it was getting harder to work.

Maggie's heart pounded faster when she saw Oliver stumble and catch himself on Hero.

"Oliver," she said, "please go in the house."

Oliver stood and folded his arms. "I want to help."

Maggie was surprised to find Jake suddenly at her side. He whispered, "Maggie, he needs to feel useful right now. I'll work beside him, if that lessens your worries."

Maggie nodded.

Jake's voice boomed. "Come on, son, let's work together on the other end of the sheeting from your mom and Gram, Okay?"

A smile spread across Oliver's face, and he gave a thumbs-up.

Jake was right. Maggie coddled Oliver too much. She knew that.

They all continued to work hard. When Maggie checked on Oliver, she was amazed to see Hero grabbing a grommet in his teeth and pulling the sheeting alongside the boy.

Thunder boomed. Too close now.

Maggie stood. She knew they'd done all they could. And if Jake hadn't been there, she didn't know how much more wouldn't be done at this point.

She called out for everyone to head into the house.

"I'll check the generator first," said Jake.

Once inside, safe from the storm and in dry clothes, they met in the living room. No one talked much as they listened to the fierce wind and driving rain.

Exhausted, Oliver soon fell asleep with his head on Gram's lap. Hero snored on the floor near her feet.

Zoe went upstairs to lie down on the bed and relax her back.

Gram, Jake and Maggie were too geared up to sleep. They listened as the storms raged. With the storm shutters closed, they couldn't see what was happening outside. Maggie thought it was probably just as well. The noise was loud as the rain pounded against the house.

The three of them sat quietly. Maggie jumped when she heard the thunder. How Oliver and Zoe were sleeping through it all baffled her. They must be more exhausted than she was.

After a few more hours, all was quiet outside. The news didn't say whether all of the storms had moved through their area.

Maggie felt like they collectively held their breaths until Jake stood up and paced the room.

"What do you think?" he asked.

"I say we check it out after something to eat," said Maggie. Even if that meant waking the others up.

"Praise be, that generator ran all night," said Gram as she shifted and tried to stretch.

Oliver and Hero both yawned at the same time.

Zoe came downstairs and declared herself as good as new. Maggie saw she was moving with more ease than last night.

"What does everyone think about peanut butter and jelly sandwiches for breakfast?" Maggie asked.

Jake laughed. "The sooner we eat, the sooner we see what's happened!"

As Maggie stepped off the porch, Jake took her hand.

The sky was cloudless and a soggy landscape greeted them. Tree limbs and debris littered the ground. Puddles of standing water stood in low-lying spots. The air smelled damp and musty.

Most importantly, looking out over the flower fields, they saw the sheeting held and the greenhouses were secure.

Jake was glad to see Maggie smile. Her face had been etched with worry all night.

"We couldn't have done this without you here," she said.

"It's true, Jake," Gram said as she joined them.

"I had a hard time keeping up," Zoe said.

"Stop," Maggie said. "You all helped me so much. I was flagging too. No one could keep up with Gram though!"

"True," said Jake as he hugged a blushing Gram.

Hero and Oliver came bounding down the porch stairs.

"And we also have these two to thank for the successful outcome!" Jake declared.

Oliver stopped. His eyes widened. "M-Mom?" he said as he looked at Maggie.

Maggie knelt down on one knee. "We couldn't have done it without you, honey," she said.

Oliver threw his arms around her in a big hug.

Everyone pitched in to restore the farm back to its natural state. The ground was too soggy to bring anything out from the barn, so Jake joined the others at the edge of the row of smaller dahlias.

A collective sigh of relief filled the air until Gram's phone rang.

"Oh no, how bad is it?" asked Gram.

Maggie and Jake looked at each other.

Once the call ended, Gram looked at them with tears in her eyes. "There was some damage in town as you'd imagine. And Jake, your choir member Carol is in the hospital. She'll be all right, but her house is in need of repair. Fortunately, her husband, Brian, thinks the insurance will cover it."

Jake sent up a prayer of thanks that Carol would be all right.

Even though he was bone tired, he wanted to see Carol for himself and to be there for Brian. They had been there for him and Maggie when she had her PTSD attack in the park.

At the hospital, Carol and Brian were happy to see Jake.

"I heard what happened from Gram and came right over," Jake said. "Maggie will be visiting soon, she's with Oliver and the family."

"Oh, we totally understand, Jake. And we appreciate you coming right over," said Carol.

"We really do," said Brian and hugged him. "How did you all make out at the flower farm?"

"We got some damage but we all made sure to get things ready before the storm hit and that helped a lot. We have repairs to do but we're all right," Jake said. "Listen, anything I can do to help at your place, you let me know," he added.

Brian looked at Carol, who had tears in her eyes. "Jake, I appreciate that," Brian said. "What's important is we all made it through, thanks to God. The place will be all right. The same goes for you too, if you need help."

Jake nodded. He was so blessed to know this couple.

"I'm going to be all right too, don't you worry," Carol said. "It'll take some time to heal, the doctors say. And I'll be in these casts for a while," she said, pointing to her leg and arm.

"And she better get used to being spoiled rotten," Brian added, winking at his wife.

Jake smiled as Carol blushed.

"But Jake, this sure puts you in a bind, doesn't it? There will be a real gap in the alto section of the choir," said Carol.

"That's nothing for you to worry about," said Jake. "You just concentrate on healing."

Jake didn't stay much longer as he didn't want to tire Carol out. He also knew she'd have more visitors and he wanted the couple to have some quiet, restful time together.

As he walked to the truck, he vowed to make sure he brought something special when he visited next. Though he bet when Gram, Zoe and Maggie visited, there would be some homemade treats.

Driving home, he thought about what Carol had said. Her alto voice provided a rich harmony between the soprano and tenor voices.

Practice was coming up to prepare for the important Sunday service. People would want to gather together after Hurricane Duncan, to pray for everyone.

He'd hear the difference in the worship songs but maybe the congregation wouldn't.

Two days later, Jake busied himself with cleaning up the rest of the storm debris. There was a lot to do. The wedding was only a couple of weeks away.

He wheeled supplies from the barn to work on the gazebo. He found Oliver and Hero waiting for him. They unloaded everything onto the plywood lying atop the sawhorses.

Two hours later, the gazebo was built and ready for painting. It would be perfect for wedding photography on the farm. He was sure Maggie would do a beautiful job of enhancing it with flowers.

Jake started humming then broke into singing "What a Friend We Have in Jesus." Soon Oliver accompanied him word for word—in his *alto* vocal range.

Should he ask Oliver to sing at this Sunday's service?

"Oliver, I have a question for you. You can say no or not right now if you want to. That would be fine." Jake proceeded with some trepidation.

Oliver looked at him with a quizzical expression.

"Remember when we talked about you possibly singing in the choir?" Jake asked.

Oliver nodded.

"Well, one of my choir singers won't be able to sing on Sunday. And your vocal range is the same as hers. I was wondering—"

"You—you want m-me to s-sing?" Oliver's eyes were wide as he stumbled backward.

Jake drew in a deep breath and let it out. "Only if you want to try. Practice is tomorrow if you want to see how you feel about it. Only if you're comfortable, though," Jake reassured him.

Oliver was silent as he patted Hero repeatedly.

Jake didn't want to pressure him, so, humming softly, he turned back to priming the gazebo for paint.

A few minutes passed, and Oliver tugged on the sleeve of his denim shirt.

"I—I—I think I—I—I'd like to try."

"That's wonderful, Oliver. Trying is very brave. See how you like it. I'll let the others know," said Jake with a broad smile.

He could tell Oliver was a little anxious, but his courage seemed to be winning.

"Now, let's get back to work," Jake said with a quick pat on Oliver's knee.

The next morning, Jake called Maggie, hoping she could talk freely.

"He's been up since the sun rose," Maggie said.

"Is that good or bad?" Jake asked.

"I'd say good. He's been practicing, gargling water and trying on multiple changes of clothes so far. He told me he was going to sing with grown-ups today. And he asked if I could make brownies to bring for everyone!" Maggie laughed.

"Can you?" Jake asked. "I think that's a great idea." He laughed.

"So you approve of his possible bribery for approval?" Maggie asked.

Seeing the smile on her face, he said, "Well, I did mention that we usually hang out after the practice and there are usually treats."

"Hmm, I may have to check this out and see just what is going on—singing, treats, sounds like fun!" declared Maggie.

"Seriously, would you feel better if you were there? Would Oliver? I'm bringing Hero. He's been there before, and the choir loves him," Jake said.

"I hadn't thought about going, but now that you mention it..."

"We could all ride together," Jake suggested.

Maggie grinned and nodded. "Sounds like a plan."

The next day, on their way to rehearsal, he kept the back window of the pickup open so Hero didn't feel excluded in the truck bed with Maggie and Oliver in the cab. It didn't seem to bother him at all. At times he poked his nose in and bumped Oliver's head, which started a fit of giggles. And at the last stoplight before the church, Hero let out a howl. It drew the attention and laughter of people walking on the sidewalk and sitting in the car next to them.

"He's practicing for the choir," Maggie told them.

As soon as they pulled into the parking lot and Jake shut off the engine, two of the choir members came over to greet them. Oliver looked very much at ease as he and Hero walked in with them, leaving Jake and Maggie trailing behind.

"I can't believe this is working out so well," said Maggie.

The rehearsal went well. And Maggie's brownies were a big hit. She promised to send more homemade treats in the future.

One big difference between Oliver singing with the choir and singing at home was he closed his eyes. He checked out where Hero was before each song then sang his little heart out. Jake decided not to mention the difference to Oliver. If that was how he was more comfortable, it was all good.

And Jake was amazed that Oliver knew all the songs. Granted he'd picked more well-known songs, but still he was impressed.

Maybe this would all work out.

On Sunday morning, Jake stood looking out his bedroom window. It looked to be a beautiful August morning. A cooler dry air mass from Canada had moved into southern Maine, and it was a nice respite from the usual summer humidity.

Suddenly his phone rang.

"Good morning, Jake, it's Pastor Luke. Are you ready for today?"

"I am. Good to hear from you. Is everything all right with the choir?" he asked.

"Yes, all set for today. I'll come right to the point. We have a big morning ahead of us. I was wondering if you might consider staying on as Choir Director on a full-time basis? I know it's a big ask," Pastor Luke said.

Jake smiled. Would he consider it? In his heart, he knew he

had already decided to apply for the job. He knew he wanted to stay in Sweet Springs.

"It's an honor to be asked. Thank you. I've already been giving it some thought and yes, I would like the job," Jake said.

"Excellent. I'm very happy about this and I know others in the community will be too," said Pastor Luke.

"I couldn't be more happy about it, myself," Jake replied.

"Good. We'll announce it today if you're ready. Is that all right with you? Good news today will be welcome," said the pastor.

"Yes, that's fine with me," said Jake, "and thank you again."

Now, if he could just keep the secret from Maggie, Oliver, Gram and Zoe until church later.

Joining everyone in the kitchen, Jake kept checking the time and looking out the window. Maggie and Oliver weren't expected at the house but he hoped they'd show up. He was anxious to know how things were shaping up with Oliver. Singing with the choir in front of Maggie and Hero was one thing but in front of rows of parishioners was another.

"Why don't you just go down there, Jake?" said Zoe before she speared another forkful of Gram's banana nut pancakes.

Jake drew in a deep breath.

"Zoe, this is a big day for everyone. Don't tease your brother!" reprimanded Gram.

Jake loved the sound of his and Zoe's shared laughter.

"We're not teenagers, Gram," said Zoe.

"Never know it with you two," Gram declared with a smile. "And just so you know, Jake, I called Maggie earlier. And everything is fine. Oliver is doing well."

Jake breathed a sigh of relief.

The first time he saw Oliver that morning was in the church parking lot. Hero immediately found him, as did several members of the choir. They all walked in the side door of the church together.

Oliver caught Jake's attention as he waved and gave a thumbs-up.

Jake loved it when a plan came together.

Pastor Luke was in on the surprise Jake had planned for his family during the service today. The choir was talkative when he entered the rehearsal room. Immediately he sought out Oliver, who, thankfully, wasn't standing off by himself. Two of the members were patiently listening to him describe the storm at the flower farm.

He relaxed. And before he knew it, it was time to enter the sanctuary.

Oliver sought him out. "Where w-w-will Hero be—be?" he asked with a hint of a tremble in his voice.

"Front row, with your mom. Are you okay with that? Do you still want to do this? Remember, only if you feel comfortable," Jake said.

"I—I—I'm g-g-good," replied Oliver and reached for Jake's hand as they left the room.

Jake gave it a gentle squeeze and held back his tears. He loved this sweet son of his so much.

# Chapter Seventeen

Maggie sat in the front row of Old Grace Church. Gram held one hand and Zoe the other. Hero sat firmly planted at her feet. She kept telling herself all would be well as she prayed for Oliver's success.

The choir members entered and took their positions. Oliver entered holding Jake's hand then let go when Jake led him to his position at the front of the choir. She felt Hero wiggle a bit.

Jake turned to face the congregation. He smiled and nodded to everyone before turning back to the choir. She knew that Jake was about to begin the service with the worship song that Oliver knew best. Maggie glanced at Oliver at the same time that Jake did.

Oliver was wide-eyed and pale. Very pale.

Jake stood still.

Should she go up there? She felt Hero stand up and head toward the choir.

Maggie could tell when Jake heard the click of Hero's paws behind him on the church floor. He turned as Hero brushed against Jake's leg then pushed in beside Oliver and sat down.

A tremulous smile slowly appeared on Oliver's face. Maggie, a hand resting on her chest, saw that Oliver's color was returning.

With one hand on Hero, Oliver looked up at Jake and nodded.

At that moment, Maggie hoped Jake would trust Oliver just as she had done in the flower field during the storm.

Jake cued the choir to begin singing. Oliver closed his eyes and sang every word strong and true. The community stood and joined in. Maggie soaked in the strong feeling of healing and unity that spread throughout the sanctuary.

The theme of the sermon that day was redemption and forgiveness. Maggie felt God was speaking directly to her, Jake, Zoe and Gram through Pastor Luke's words.

Memories of the summer since Jake arrived flowed through her. What they'd shared. What he'd done for her, Oliver and others. When he kissed her. The support of her wedding venue dreams. His love had shown through in all he'd said and done since his return. Jake was returning to Kansas soon. *Let go and let God.* She was still a work in progress on that one. It would be difficult, no doubt about it.

Maggie closed her eyes for the choir's next song and tried to focus in on Oliver's voice. She let his words, without any stuttering, fill her and wrap around her. He was Jake's son as well as hers. They'd bonded so much already. Yes, it was time to reveal the truth. Jake had been patient long enough.

Zoe nudged Maggie. Jake was looking directly at them as he stood next to Pastor Luke at the podium.

"Our choir director, Jake Madison, has an announcement to make." The pastor stepped aside.

"Good morning, everyone! This position was supposed to only be temporary, but Pastor Luke has asked me to stay on as full-time choir director. I'm happy to say that I've accepted."

Clapping ensued followed by laughter. Oliver ran off the stage with Hero at his heels and threw his arms around his mother. "He's st-st-staying, M-Mom!" Oliver shouted.

Maggie looked at Jake, whose smile lit up the room. He said to her, "I guess this is a good thing!"

"A very good thing," she replied with tears in her eyes. She joined Oliver, Hero, Zoe and Gram as they made their way to Jake.

After the church service was over, the family gathered at Gram's house for lunch.

Maggie loved seeing Jake so fully accepted into the Sweet Springs community. His friends Matt, Brian, and others in the congregation had come over with handshakes, hugs and pats on the back as he made his way to Gram's truck.

At home, Gram was determined to keep the celebration going. She enveloped Jake in a warm hug. "It's so good to know you're staying, Jake. I'm so happy He listened to my prayers. You're right where you should be. I truly believe that," she said.

Maggie blushed a deep pink when he looked at her and said, "I believe that too, Gram."

Oliver zoomed by them with Hero. He was clearly running off nervous energy from the day's events.

"Maybe you both should go outside," Maggie suggested.

Maggie thought Zoe looked happy as well. She laughed as boy and dog headed out the door just before she headed outside with the tray of cookies and lemonade for everyone to enjoy on the porch.

Maggie heard Jake speaking to Zoe. "I have something I want to talk to you about outside," he said.

Zoe's forehead crinkled. "Sounds serious."

Jake smiled. "It's something good, I promise," he said. Then Jake walked over to Maggie.

"I'm especially glad you're happy I'm staying on here," he said.

"Oh, I am. No doubt about that," she said softly.

Before he could respond, Oliver ran in the front door and said, "Gram-m wants m-me to bring out some more c-c-cookies!"

"Are you sure that's true, young man?" Maggie asked with a grin.

"You're not just trying to get some extra cookies, are you?" Jake teased.

Oliver laughed and shook his head. "It's t-t-true."

Jake winked at Maggie as she and Oliver headed to the kitchen.

Jake joined Gram and Zoe on the porch. She had to admit that she was curious to hear what Jake wanted to talk to Zoe about.

Oliver delivered the cookies to Gram. She gave him a cookie, and he ran down the steps with Hero alongside.

"Okay, spill, Jake, what do you want to talk about?" Zoe asked.

Jake cleared his throat. "Zoe, you have sacrificed so much for this family. You put your own life on hold."

"Phooey, nothing I didn't want to do," said Zoe.

Jake continued, "I think it's time for you to pursue your dreams of trick riding and rodeos or whatever else your heart wants. I have some money set aside for whatever you choose to do."

Maggie watched Jake draw in a deep breath. He was clearly relieved at saying what he wanted to say. She and Gram remained silent.

"Jake," Zoe said, "that's wonderful of you. It really is. But you don't have to do that. I love you, and you have nothing to make up for, if that's what you're thinking."

"Thank you for that, Zoe." Jake's voice broke.

Zoe hesitated. "We haven't talked about the past, when it was just the three of us—you, me and Paul—after our father left. But I know you took rough jobs so we could have food. I saw the bruises—" She started to cry.

Maggie realized she had never seen her best friend cry.

Jake held up his hand. "Zoe. We don't need to go there. I

didn't know you knew about that. It's all in the past. What I'm trying to say is that you've been here for Gram, this farm, Maggie and Oliver."

Maggie's heart beat faster.

Gram spoke up, "Jake, you have a heart of gold, and don't you forget it." Maggie reached over and took Gram's hand.

"The thing is, there's money for whatever you want to do, Zoe, whenever you decide to do it," Jake said.

Zoe got up and hugged her brother. "Thank you for caring so much about me. All of you. All the time. I feel it, I really do," Zoe said. "I'm going to head to my room for a bit. It's been a big day." She looked directly at Jake. "One of the best days, knowing my brother is staying home—*where he belongs*," she said, emphasizing the last part.

Gram stood up. "I think that's a fine idea. I might lie down, as well. You made me feel happy and proud and blessed all at once today, my boy," she said and kissed the top of his head as she went by.

Jake turned to Maggie. "I think that went well, don't you?"

"I know it did," Maggie assured him.

"What did you want to talk to me about?" Jake asked her.

"It can wait until tomorrow," she said quietly.

They sat there holding hands and offered up prayers of thanks for everything that happened.

He cupped her face in his hands and looked into her eyes. He gently touched his lips to hers in a sweet kiss. It felt like the past, the present and the future all rolled into one.

The next day, Jake felt like he was home. He'd searched for it long enough, and here it was. And he felt good, really good.

Downstairs, the celebration of yesterday was still going. Gram was up cooking. A batch of blueberry muffins sat on the counter. The waffle mix was out. Fresh flowers in a glass vase were on the kitchen table.

Maggie's first wedding was coming up. He needed to coordinate with Matt on the carriage surprise. How he managed to keep this project from Gram, Zoe and Maggie was a mystery to him. And it just had to stay that way a little longer.

Jake went out onto the porch and called Pastor Joe in Kansas.

He'd missed his friend's hearty laugh. "By the sounds of all that's happened, the return home has been good for you, Jake. We'll figure out how to get your belongings to you there in Maine."

"I feel it was truly meant to be that I returned," Jake said. "It hasn't all been easy. To be honest, I'm still working on forgiving myself for the past. I do know He has forgiven me. My family has forgiven me too." Jake rubbed his neck. "And I'm grateful for another chance with Maggie and to get to know my son."

"All I can say, Jake, is that I hope you do forgive yourself," Pastor Joe said. "I see a good man doing good things according to God's plan. I'm proud to call you my friend."

Jake felt warmed by the words. He was glad his good friend deemed his behavior worthy of respect.

When the call ended, Gram joined him on the porch with two coffees. They mostly sat in silence. Every once in a while, Gram would reach over and pat his knee, and they'd both smile.

Jake's cell phone rang. It was Maggie. "Jake, I have something I'd like to talk to you about when you have a moment."

"How about now? I can meet you at your place," he suggested.

When he arrived a few minutes later, Maggie seemed nervous. She fidgeted and asked him to sit down. He started to sit down at the kitchen table. Then she suggested the living room. Then he caught her looking back at the chair in the kitchen.

"Mags, what's up?" he asked.

She looked pretty in a white dress with pink flowers. Jake drew her into his arms. She smelled as beautiful as she looked.

He'd never get over being grateful at being able to hold her like this.

"Do you have something to tell me?" he asked.

"More like something to ask you?" she answered.

"Okay, well, I'm having a hard time reading your mind, but I can try harder." Jake closed his eyes and scrunched his face up.

Maggie giggled nervously.

"I want you to know… I think I'm ready… I think we should… Oh, this isn't going well," Maggie said, exasperated.

"Mags?"

"I think—if you want to—we should tell Oliver you're his father." Maggie waited.

"I…" Jake stammered.

"Now you're doing it," said Maggie.

"I can't tell you how many times I've dreamed of this day," said Jake, rubbing his hands on his jeans. He recalled seeing Oliver do the same thing recently.

"You realize, once we tell him, that you may be the only father he remembers," Maggie said. "He doesn't remember Paul. He's seen photos of him and heard stories."

Just like on Gram's porch the other night, he took her hands in his and they prayed on it. "We'll do the best we can with His help, Mags."

After just sitting together with two cups of tea for a few moments, Jake spoke up.

"I'm wondering if we should build up to it or just talk to him directly?"

Maggie drew in a deep breath and let it whoosh out. "You were right when you once said that Oliver is pretty perceptive. He'll know something is up if we start talking around it," said Maggie.

Jake nodded. "All we can do is explain it now with as much honesty and clarity as possible."

"Now?" Maggie repeated.

"No time like the present," Jake said as he took her hand.

Maggie called Oliver inside. Hero came in with him and promptly plopped down on the floor.

"We have something to tell you, Oliver," said Maggie.

"The truth is… Jake is your biological father," Maggie stated. "You were conceived before I married Paul. Paul was your father when you were little."

Oliver was very quiet as he sat in his chair. Jake wondered suddenly if it was too much for him. Should they have waited until he was older? Maybe this would set him back?

Jake took Maggie's hand in his.

Oliver looked at their clasped hands and then at Jake.

"You're n-n-not my Uncle J-J-Jake?" he asked. "I had two fathers?"

"That's right. I'm your father, and I'm really happy about that," he said honestly.

Jake fought back his tears.

Oliver hesitated. "M-M-Mom, are you ha-ha-happy about this?"

Maggie with tears in her eyes as well said, "I am."

Oliver paused again before looking at Jake. "I—I already think of you th-that way. You c-called me s-son during the st-st-storm."

Maggie and Jake both smiled.

"C-c-can I call you…Dad?" Oliver asked Jake.

"Yes. I'd be honored if you did that. But only if you want to, okay?"

Oliver joined Maggie and Jake on the couch.

Oliver said, "I—I love you both. I'm going to rem-member this m-moment forever."

They all hugged each other close.

# *Epilogue*

A beautiful sunny Maine day set the perfect stage for the wedding of Nate and Louise. The first wedding of Maggie's new Maine Bliss wedding venue.

Maggie and Zoe had planned everything down to the last detail. The flower decorations garnered a lot of attention. The white twinkle lights and drapery were beautiful.

Jake's arched podium where Nate waited patiently for his bride was decked out in beautiful dahlias and assorted asters, cosmos and zinnias.

Where was the bride?

Zoe had insisted on being the one to make sure she was ready to walk down the aisle.

Where was Zoe?

And where was Jake? He wasn't sitting next to Gram.

And where was Oliver?

The string quartet began. Just as Maggie thought she should make a motion to stop them, everyone stood.

Oohs and ahhs announced the arrival of a beautiful white Cinderella carriage drawn by Zoe's horse, Lucky Lady.

Zoe and Oliver sat on the driver's bench seat. Louise sat in the back with her dahlia bouquet. Lucky Lady looked happy but a bit awkward in her new role.

The carriage pulled up to the red carpet, and Louise stepped out. Beaming, she looked toward Nate, her groom. The meadowsweet and dahlia flower crown that Maggie designed for her looked beautiful atop her head.

Jake came up quietly beside Maggie and whispered, "Surprise!"

"You?" She looked at him with tears in her eyes.

"And Matt. And Oliver. I told Zoe yesterday. She had a grand time decking out Lucky Lady today," Jake said.

Maggie wiped away a tear. "This is such a gift. A wonderful surprise!"

Maggie knew with all her heart that she was truly blessed to have this man in her life. "Thank you. For the surprise of the carriage. And for making my dreams come true!"

Later, a cool breeze carried the honey-vanilla scent of the sweet autumn clematis to Gram's porch where Maggie sat with the family after the wedding.

It seemed like everyone who attended had gushed to Maggie and Zoe about how wonderful the wedding and reception had been. Maggie held onto that warm happy feeling all day and well into the evening.

Weddings definitely made her happy. Her favorite part though was seeing Louise and Nate so happy.

"That carriage is so beautiful," Gram said. "When you advertise the wedding venue, Maggie, be sure to include a photo of it. I'm sure it'll be a big draw."

"It already is," said Maggie. "We have three more weddings booked!"

Jake cleared his throat. "Three more?"

Oliver interjected. "M-Mom! Dad has s-s-something to ask you!"

Jake stood in front of Maggie, took off his Stetson and set it atop Oliver's head as the boy grinned up at him.

Then Jake fished out a small purple velvet box from his pocket.

"Speaking of weddings, don't you think we should book ours while there are still some spots left on the calendar?" he asked as he knelt down on one knee.

Not waiting for an answer, he opened the box slowly. Maggie noticed his fingers trembled.

Her heart beat faster.

"Maggie, I may have messed up our yesterdays. I can't change the past. I know I'll always be grateful that Paul was there for you and Oliver," said Jake with a hitch in his voice. "I'm asking you now to share all our tomorrows. You're the love of my life and—"

"I love you too," Maggie said. She extended her hand. Jake slipped a gold band with a round brilliant-cut diamond on her finger.

"I love it," she said. With tears in her eyes, she threw her arms around his neck and kissed him.

Gram laughed. "I'm guessing that's a yes."

Hero barked.

Everyone laughed.

Oliver piped up. "Gram, I—I'm so lucky. Hero and I—I have the b-best mom and dad in the whole world."

"Yes, it's true," Gram said.

Maggie saw the tears of joy as everyone gathered around to congratulate her and Jake. Even Hero felt the excitement. He took turns bumping each person's leg for a pat on the head.

Jake caught Maggie's attention and walked toward her. Gathering her in his arms, he held her tight.

"I have one more surprise," he said. "I have some plans I'd like you to look at for a home for us near the stone wall beyond Gram's house. I'm thinking it should have some wide window sills for herbs in the kitchen and a bay window for a Christmas tree in the living room."

Maggie's eyes filled will tears. "You remembered," she said softly.

"Yes, those were the things you dreamed of that day in the kitchen," Jake said, his voice husky with emotion.

Maggie's heart was full. She felt safe and secure in her life with Oliver and the man she'd always loved.

* * * * *

Dear Reader,

Hello! Thank you for reading my debut novel with Love Inspired!

Sometimes we make decisions that take us away from our loved ones and it's hard to return. Not everyone gets a second chance. It took Jake Madison years to return home. Only after he met a pastor in Kansas did Jake finally open his heart to the Lord. And only after he returns home can he earn forgiveness from his sister, grandmother—and from his first love, Maggie.

Writing this story was a joy. I was drawn into the world of Maine flower farms while doing research for Maggie's flower business. Learning about the state's seasonal flowers continues to fascinate me.

I've been blessed to share my life with many wonderful dogs over the years. Hero is Jake's faithful canine companion and is an integral part of Oliver's journey. I hope you fell in love with Hero as much as I did while writing the story!

Thank you for following Jake and Maggie's story as it unfolded. I hope you enjoyed their journey. You can find me on Facebook at Author Vera Smetzer.

Thank you,
*Vera*